Spouses & Other Crimes

"In this wittily titled, career-spanning collection, Andrew Coburn uncovers and lays bare the compromises and motivations that push us, stumbling, through the mire of daily life, whether in the backwaters of hometowns or out there in a wider world. We open with a story of a small town back in the 1960s, a disturbing story, transportable to any decade, anywhere. The viewpoint of a 12-year-old boy melds, seamlessly, into that of the boy now become a man, struck with the realization that the past is coming back to threaten a terrible disruption. The eponymous anti-hero, Charlie, once 'a fifty-year-old slip of a fellow, brittle and bird-like, created, it would seem, out of chewed chicken bones," returns, chillingly: 'sugar-coated now, with little blue eyes like a pervert's.'

"Coburn proceeds to take us on journeys of, at best, questionable motives. Broken dreams, stained war records, nuggets of hope built around a family get-together—this is human life as we know it to be. Our final stop is the enigmatic 'Plum Island' where taciturn men gather to fish in futility. It's a closing vignette that hints at so much, and leaves so many questions nagging at our brains. Perhaps the solution lies in the choice we make every day, the simple imperative to 'Carry on, son.'

"This is long overdue rounding up of some of the best short fiction of one of America's most stylish writers. Dip in cautiously; digest with slow relish."

—ALLEN ASHLEY
ESSAYIST, AWARD-WINNING
LONDON ANTHOLOGIST

PRAISE FOR SPOUSES & OTHER CRIMES

"With *Spouses & Other Crimes,* Andrew Coburn proves my long held belief that whether he's writing crime fiction or literary fiction, he is a major American writer, a stylist and social observer of the first rank."
—Ed Gorman, author of the "Sam McCain" series

"Blunt, quirky, knowing, always unsettling, Coburn's stories are as authentic as fiction gets. Places well known and long gone, losses sudden and slow, the inexplicable actions of everyday people struggling in a nonsensical world stay with you each time you put the book down until you pick it up again, which you assuredly will do."
—R. C. Binstock, author of *Tree of Heaven,* *The Soldier* and *Swift River*

"These stories are mordantly funny, scathing and wise. The women characters, particularly, have an unblinkered view of their lives that is refreshingly unsentimental and adult. No happy endings here, just perfect ones."
—Michael Nava, author of *The City of Palaces*

"Written in language that is precise yet slippery—and as telling in what it omits as what it says—Andrew Coburn's often strangely erotic stories lead us again and again into a quicksand of surprise, taking us under the edges of his characters, exposing the jagged corners of their lives."
—John Harvey, author of the "Charlie Resnick" series

"A wonderful collection by one of those rare writers able to weave the gritty and the sublime. Andrew Coburn's sure touch captures all that it means to be fully engaged in life. In his character's pitch-perfect voices, you hear the intensity, pleasure and raw emotions of real relationships."
—Mary McGarry Morris, *A Dangerous Woman,* *Songs in Ordinary Time*

SPOUSES

& OTHER CRIMES

WORKS BY ANDREW COBURN

In order of publication

Novels
The Trespassers
The Babysitter
Off Duty
Company Secrets
Widow's Walk

The Sweetheart Trilogy
Sweetheart; Love Nest; Goldilocks
The Bensington Novels
No Way Home; Voices in the Dark

Birthright
On the Loose

Novella
My Father's Daughter

Short stories
Spouses & Other Crimes

SPOUSES
& OTHER CRIMES
SHORT STORIES BY
ANDREW COBURN

Stark House Press • Eureka California

SPOUSES & OTHER CRIMES
Published by Stark House Press
1315 H Street
Eureka, CA 95501, USA
griffinskye3@sbcglobal.net
www.starkhousepress.com

Early versions of the following pieces made their initial appearance
in the publications listed below.
"Charlie Judd": *Transatlantic Review*, June 1964
"Bang Bang" (as "Spouses"): *The Summerset Review*, Winter 2007
"Wide World of War": *Consequence Magazine*, 2010
"Katie Couric": *Arcadia Magazine* 2011
"The Christmas Clara Cried": *Eclectica Magazine*, October/November 2010
"Ginger": *Waccamaw Journal*, Spring 2009
"George W. Bush": *Wheelhouse Magazine*, Summer 2007
"Jocelyn": *The Massachusetts Review*, Winter 2009/10
"A Woolf in Vita's Clothing": *Underground Voices*, April 2007
"Plum Island": *Contrary Magazine*, Winter 2006
"Mrs. Comeau" appears here for the first time.

"About Andrew Coburn" © 2014 by Rick Ollerman
All rights reserved

ISBN: 1-933586-69-9
ISBN-13: 978-1-933586-69-4

Cover design and layout by Mark Shepard, WWW.SHEPGRAPHICS.COM
Proofreading by Rick Ollerman

First Stark House Press Edition: September 2014
FIRST EDITION

CONTENTS

CONTENTS

ABOUT ANDREW COBURN

by Rick Ollerman

It's said that writers can be good at short stories or good at novels but rarely good at both; it's said so often it could even be true. However we define novels—character studies on the way to climax and denouement, page-turning narratives of plot device, deeper studies of theme and insights into life and humanity, flat out mind-striking entertainment, whatever—they strive to entertain. As do short stories, but without the luxury or curse of length, subtext—the things that are said without being written—becomes a much more important tool for the author to master in order to make his point. In a short story, this comes faster and sharper than in a novel.

Short stories may have more in common with poems than they do with novels. If a poem is a piece where every word must count, then every word wants to be the right word, the perfect word. A poem might be evocative, informative, sensual; it might be as alive as a single something that flares into existence, then disappears, leaving an imprint on the conscious mind. It might be a hummingbird that zooms past your head, there and gone, almost unrecognizable until that moment later when you realize what it was.

Short stories can do that: evoke, stimulate; use not only the perfect word in its precise, perfect spot, but use characters as word poems unto themselves.

Andrew Coburn was born in Exeter, New Hampshire in 1932. He went into the Army out of high school at age 18, serving time in Frankfurt. After his time in the service, he attended Suffolk University and became an award-winning crime journalist in Massachusetts. He covered organized crime and for a while carried a hand gun after learning a contract had been put out against his life.

He turned this experience to fiction. In 1965 he received the Eugene Saxton Fellowship—earlier recipients included James Baldwin and Rachel Carson—and published his first novel, *The Trespassers*, in 1974.

Known for his haunting prose about crime in the towns outside of Boston, Coburn began a trilogy with the novel *Sweetheart* in 1985; continued in 1987 with *Love Nest*; and concluded with *Goldilocks* in 1989. Nominated for the Mystery Writers of America's Edgar Allan Poe award for Best Novel, *Goldilocks* gave way to *Black Cherry Blues*, the third entry in James Lee Burke's Dave Robicheaux series. Burke, like Coburn, is known for the lyrical use of language and staggering sentences that transcend the genres—mystery; thriller; psychological suspense— that they fill in the marketplace. Whatever they write about, the work itself is beautiful, even in most cases where it involves a subject as ugly as crime.

Author Ed Gorman says, "Andrew Coburn writes page-turners. A special kind of page-turner." He also praises his "authenticity," saying that "Andrew has BEEN THERE." Of his novel, 2006's *On the Loose*, Gorman says:

"I've been saying for years that the single most neglected major crime fiction writer in the United States is Andrew Coburn. And here he is with a new novel to prove me right again. I've spent two days trying to think of a tidy way to describe *On the Loose* and thus far my best shot is to imagine a collaboration between John D. MacDonald and Ruth Rendell. MacDonald for the page-turning excitement of following the most unique serial killer since *The Bad Seed* and Rendell for [the quirky characters]."

Gorman continues. "And the writing itself. Coburn plays all the instruments in the orchestra... lyrical, funny, solemn, sarcastic, violent, terrifying and human in a way page-turners rarely are."

High praise indeed. If Andrew Coburn is one of the unrecognized gems of the literary world, he certainly leaves his mark on those who discover his work.

In addition to his "Sweetheart Trilogy," Coburn's *No Way Home* (1992) and *Voices in the Dark* (1994) form a duology: tales of small-town Bensington, Massachusetts, "under pressure," says *Publishers Weekly* of the first, "from city and state politics." Of the companion novel: "This slick, suspenseful thriller, the second appearance [...] of James Morgan, police chief of the seemingly peaceful Boston suburb of Bensington, begins with a suspicious death—and, as luck would have it, a self-confessed murderer. [...] A somber conclusion at a private care facility involves the abandoned elders of Bensington families and underscores the long line of loneliness and dreary existence often at the core of small-town life."

That last sentence leads us to one of the strengths of Coburn's work. He looks at the quiet events below the surface of what appear to be typical American suburbs; he examines his characters deeply, and knows what moves them, makes them feel, imbues them with who they are.

In *Spouses & Other Crimes*, the first short story collection of his long career, Coburn tips his novels over to tell stories, not of crime per se, but of their hurt. Indeed, in this case, the use of the word "crimes" in the title might be a euphemism for the word "pain." The tales he tells here are of the different forms of despair and longing, typically quiet, some unrecognized by the characters themselves. Dig a bit, and we all know, to one degree or another, these feelings in ourselves.

So these are not stories of the hunt for the solution to the dark and depraved. Here, the conflicts flare up between wants and desires and lives not yet turned true. The stories collected here originally appeared in various publications from 1964 through 2011; one, previously unpublished, appears here for the first time. If we look at the collection as the lifespan of a human being, the first story, "Charlie Judd," centers on a twelve-year-old boy seeing his future in an encounter with a fifty-year-old man. It is a version of a certain kind of growing up; not troubled, exactly, but shadowed with omen and portent.

The last story, "Plum Island," tells of another such encounter, terminating the line begun with "Charlie Judd." Two fishermen talk: one younger, well equipped; the other older, angling with old, inappropriate gear; and the difference speaks volumes.

Darkness arrives quickly. We can no longer see where we have cast our lines. Nearby a fish is making its final argument with a hook baited by one of the other fishermen .The old man wonders aloud about the guilt of a fish that gives itself up so easily.

"Listen," he says and tells me about the woman's child, a boy of four, who buried a dead bird and exhumed it a day later, upset because it hadn't risen. Then he talks about the woman's face, which eventually gave out a silent message. "Ask me anything. I have no answers."

[...] He reels in his line. No bait left on the hook, which is how he wants it. He separates the pole into two pieces. His box of sandworms is mine if I want it. He must return to Boston. Here at Plum Island, where things become lost forever in the sand or washed away with the tide, the world is ageless, all of a piece, fish and fisherman one, the fishermen interchangeable, ghosts of other generations. He and I are one, our age difference blurred.

The first story is longer, the young narrator's life laid out before him; the last story, shorter, is about endings. In between is a cycle of stories that seem to age the way we do, each in our own manner, moving with the irregular phases of lives lived with faults, with pain, with regret, with mistakes.

This gives a poem-like structure to the collection as a whole; it's also one story, the story of a single metaphorical life cycle, not only of one person, but of a collection of people who are, in some ways, similar to each other. Or to us, the readers of the stories. There's a recurring character, a Dr. Wall who does something important: he listens, his welcoming ear a balm for clients in need of help, desperate for answers though he has few to give. In Coburn, we make our way through our lives more or less on our own. We can look for help from somewhere else, and while it may be soothing to look, we don't necessarily find it.

There's poetry in the individual stories themselves. In "Ginger," a lost and talented writer leaves a trail of wrong men behind before she finds real love with perhaps the most damaged man she knows, the editor at the magazine where she works. And she knows she has to leave.

Standing on the Cambridge side of the Charles River, against a chill fall wind that sounded like a holler for help and would've bowled her over had she not clutched the rail, she began composing her last piece for *Boston World*. The first line struck a mood.

November is a bone begging for a dog.

There—an exact, precise description of the exact, precise moment that Ginger, ambitious and intelligent, re-launches her search for happiness. She may not find it easily. But then, most of us don't.

Later stories show other characters looking for their second acts, as Ellen Burnside does when she and her husband come into some money and need help to make it grow. Jack O'Grady is there, but he has his own lecherous motives. Coburn gives us pain to balance the pleasure, conflict to offset opportunity.

Life does not glide smoothly for these characters in Coburn's stories. Some of his people appear similar but show different facets of pain and struggle as they chase their own elusive state of human happiness. Perhaps it can be achieved. Perhaps not. Some of us give up.

These stories that Coburn gives us are beautiful, lyrical portraits of a composite life, and there is something of an ambivalence to the collection as a whole, start to finish, that mirrors that same condition in real life.

These stories show us what it is to be human in Coburn's world. Never all the way happy, never all the way miserable, but striving to use our gifts toward an elusive *something*, salmon swimming against the current, driven to spawn. Most remarkably, though, is the beauty in which the stories are told.

November is a bone begging for a dog?

Of course it is. In Andrew Coburn's world, it has to be.

SUMMER 2014
LITTLETON, NEW HAMPSHIRE

SPOUSES
& OTHER CRIMES

CHARLIE JUDD

The sky is warm and white, sudsy with clouds. No more rain. The rain came last night and soaked the canvas chairs, which is why I'm perched on the porch rail while down below, having crept past bordering shrubs, Charlie Judd is slinking through the grass—a fifty-year-old slip of a fellow, brittle and birdlike, created, it would seem, out of chewed chicken bones. He stares up at me, shamed to tears because of the daily dirty mission his wife Leah has sent him on. This is a small town, things like this happen, so let me point out that this is two months before Charlie murders his wife in the second degree. And let me add that I'm actually sitting a good deal higher than the porch rail and can see these things.

Suddenly but not unexpectedly, Charlie's eyes fly up. "No rain, that's plain—hey, Sonny."

The name's mine, so I put up with it. With spryness, with queer hops, he mounts the steps. I wave him away from a damp deck chair he wouldn't have sat in, anyway. The idea is to learn as much as possible from me, without my grandmother knowing, about what has been going on. What was the ruckus last evening. Did my father slap my mother or did she slap him. And did my grandmother butt in? This sort of thing. According to rumor, my grandmother and Leah Judd were once like blood sisters. Now it's a toss-up as to which one, behind the other's back, is more vicious.

"Charlie," I say, trying, never succeeding, to be gentle, "let me save us both time. The whole business last night was a misunderstanding, nothing worth carrying back."

I may have embarrassed him, or he may not be listening. Leah's pantry window juts out above the shrubs, and I know she's at the window because I saw the curtains move. To save Charlie grief, I say quickly, "It was mostly my grandmother's fault because she kept hounding my father about my mother working."

This is juicy, and Charlie looks at me gratefully. It's dangerous to make

small talk with Charlie because Leah, from her window, will think I've
told him more than I have and will pound hell out of him later if she
thinks he has forgotten anything. She is tall and skinny, made out of
a single hard bone, and she has a long horse face that snorts. From *The
Newsletter*, our weekly paper, she clips out marriage and birth an-
nouncements, a splendid cross-index that gives out instant evidence
against those girls who were premature with their affection. To my
mind this is pretty filthy of Leah. I think she's sick but we all have our
ways, and that's Leah's.

"Show me your tattoo, Charlie."

He hikes his sleeve high and displays an arm that could pass for a stick
of kindling. Tattooed on the spotted skin of his biceps is *U.S. NAVY*
wreathed in roses. At least I think they're roses. The whole business
looks rather waterlogged. I've neglected to mention that Charlie always
wears blue, ordinary, blue workmen's clothes to resurrect his navy days
thirty years ago. Great times, although according to Leah, he never
stepped foot on a ship. Never even got out of boot camp.

"Beautiful, Charlie. Roll it down."

We chuckle together, as if I'm supposed to know about certain
things, fast times he had during shore leave, stuff he hasn't told me
about because of my age and all. I'm twelve and know everything,
which is the reason my attention is driven across the street. Sitting on
her steps, legs ajar, is Shirley Teller. For nickels and dimes, pennies if
they add up, she shows her privates. Charlie has had his share of peeks.

His ear is cocked as if for danger. We both can hear my grandmother moving about inside, probably brewing tea for herself. If she
knew Charlie was on the porch she'd come out and speak to him,
which would annoy Leah and gradually infuriate her.

"Charlie, do you have a nickel?"

"Not on me."

If someone, Charlie for instance, told me that Leah's frail cousin
Emma, Leah being ten years dead, would clip out the notice of my en-
gagement to Shirley, I'd call him crazy. But this is exactly what will happen. Different story having more significance later.

Charlie runs his hands over the dust-like hair on his head and smiles
at me. Sometimes we have marvelous moments of understanding. It's

as if he has pushed away all the cobwebs and hears me say, "It's all right, Charlie. I won't let anything happen to you."

Putt-putt-putt. It comes from up the street and grows louder. In a second or so the plump blue body of Ben Boitt will bolt by on a police motorcycle. Every kid in town waves to Ben, myself included. It's expected. He's already too fat for the bike, which is partly the reason they'll make him Chief.

"Hey, Ben!" My arm shoots up like a flag and flaps like one. Charlie waves too, not as vigorously since it's not expected. He has more admiration for Ben's blue than for Ben's bike and no admiration for Ben himself. Last fall, while Leah was spending six days and nights with sick cousin Emma, Charlie dressed himself in a black suit and purple shirt with a wide white tie and popped a soiled fedora on his head. I don't know where in God's name he picked up the outfit but he looked like a real out-of-town gangster type, the sort seen in Saturday matinees at the Ioka. He hung around outside Kurtz's Diner, across from the bank, as if casing it. Ben watched him like a nervous cat and finally, on the fourth or fifth evening, with a drawn .38-caliber revolver, he snuck up on Charlie and yelled, "Freeze!" Charlie whirled around with his finger on the trigger of a shiny cap pistol purchased at the dime store. Both men fired, and both missed, Charlie figuratively. The story never made *The Newsletter,* probably because Ben threatened the editor, and by some miracle the story never got back to Leah, who'd have had Charlie committed.

Across the street Tommy MacAllister approaches Shirley Teller. A full inch taller than I, he has a pasty face under coal-black hair combed in a big wet wave. Industrious to a fault, he mows lawns, hauls rubbish, delivers magazines, and runs all sorts of errands. He is holding a super-size redeemable soda bottle by the neck. With rage I watch Shirley accept it and disappear with him behind shrubs.

Charlie senses my rage but not the reason for it. He doesn't know that Tommy MacAllister, developing into a shyster real estate agent, will sell Shirley and me a seven-room Cape Cod for our growing family. Charlie moves a little closer to me. His shirt reeks of an iron. The sun, previously lolling behind billowy clouds, tears loose and strikes Charlie, scattering him. To my horror, with only particles of him visible, he seems two-thirds fictitious.

Quick raps from Leah's pantry window come as a relief. Charlie returns in full form and deciphers Leah's twisty mouth behind the glass. "She means you too, Sonny." He prances down the steps and, with an oblique tilt, crosses the lawn.

The Judd house is quiet as a tomb. No radio or television playing. Leah won't allow either in the house, a waste of time and electricity. Besides, she doesn't want Charlie exciting himself over TV commercials using sex to sell products. Her big horse face snorts down at me.

"Sit down, Sonny. Judd, get the boy a glass of water."

Charlie returns with one of her good glasses and receives a cuff on the head. He retreats and returns with a jelly jar, which he hands to her and she passes to me. While I drink lukewarm water she pulls Charlie to one side so that he can parrot what I have told him about the ruckus. Shamefacedly in chirping whispers, he does so.

"Well, what about it?" Leah says, wheeling around. "Your mother gonna still work or not?"

"It's undecided," I reply.

"If your father can't make enough, it's no business of your grandmother's. She see you come over here?"

"I don't think so."

"Who buys the groceries, your grandmother or your father?"

"My father brings them home. I imagine he pays for them."

"But you don't know for sure. What we do know is your grandmother doesn't have any money of her own. I mean, that's a solid fact, isn't it, Sonny?"

I rise to my grandmother's defense. "She gives me nickels when I ask for them."

She hits Charlie with a horsy look, and fear comes into his small blue eyes. "You just sit there a minute," she says to me and vanishes.

"Don't you worry," my eyes try to tell Charlie. "I'll take care of you."

"I think you're old enough to know about this," Leah says, bustling back with a bulging scrapbook with flaky edges. With a moistened finger she flips apart dry thick pages. Her crooked nail points to a yellowish newspaper clipping bearing the name of my father and the maiden name of my mother, the nail scrapes an inch to the right to another clipping. There it is, in black and yellow, with a penciled calculation by Leah. Either I was a five-month baby weighing nearly nine pounds or someone was up to tricks.

"Look your mother in the eyes now, if you can," Leah says.

Charlie makes a little chirping noise.

"What's ailing you?" Leah says and slaps his mouth hard enough to hurt him. Then she disappears with the scrapbook under her arm.

"She wasn't always like that," Charlie says, checking his lips for bleeding. "She was pretty once."

I nod.

"She oughtn't to have shown you that," he says.

"She oughtn't to have slapped you," I say.

"I oughtn't to have let her."

"Maybe next time you ought to stop her," I say, quite softly.

Charlie nods, "She won't do it again," he says.

We exchange a secret smile before she comes back, a log-long shadow that Charlie has already cut down.

My grandmother is setting the supper table for when my mother and father come home from work. I'm in the bathroom combing my hair first one way, then another; there's not much you can do with a cowlick bad as mine. Then I remember something and rush out to the porch, climb onto the rail, and wait. You can tell summer is mellowing because the big green tree at the Judds' house is dropping yellow leaves. I wait. I'm not trying to excuse myself, but I can well imagine the filthy fun Leah would have had with Shirley and me. Shirley is on her steps. She'll be off them soon enough. I wait. Then it comes, the God-awful bloody scream.

Mostly kids gather in the street, then neighbors, people in cars, finally Ben Boitt. My grandmother is stationed in the yard, frantic with curiosity, ordering me to go over to see what has happened. I don't budge. Finally she goes herself because now the scene is loaded. State cops, an ambulance, a *Newsletter* reporter with a camera. White-faced, his wet wave collapsing, Tommy MacAllister charges into my yard.

"Guess what! Charlie Judd murdered his wife."

"I know. Hacked her to pieces."

Popeyed, Tommy says, "How do you know? They haven't said how yet."

I could bite my tongue. I don't want him to know how high I'm sitting. "I'm guessing," I say, which, in a way, is more effective than I had hoped. Tommy will go through life suspecting I had something to do with Leah's killing.

Tommy snaps his head around. The crowd, standing in a stiff frieze, watches state cops, followed by Ben Boitt, march Charlie from the house to a marked car. He's wearing a nearly new flat cap and freshly ironed blues. They must have made him change. Before climbing into the car, he searches the crowd with a soft trusting look. Then the tiniest flicker of panic touches his face. He should've looked over here, toward the porch.

The grass in the Judds' yard, which hasn't been cut in a week, is long enough for the wind to push and shove. People still drive by to look at the Judds' house, and some stop and get out of their cars to peer through the pantry window. My grandmother has gotten over her shock and what she claims was a heart attack. My father has been extra nice to her, letting my mother stay out of work to care for her. Tommy MacAllister has put the bug in Shirley's ear that I know more than I let on. As a result she has been spending more time on my steps than on her own.

The biggest question in the county prosecutor's mind is whether Charlie is loony or not. Everyone, with the exception of Ben Boitt, wants to make it as easy as possible for him. But he's being difficult. He wants no lawyer, only me. They explain he can't have a kid defending him in a court of law. Come autumn, they all agree that Charlie will enter a plea of second-degree murder, something about provocation and no premeditation. They convict.

The sky is warm and white, sudsy with clouds. Amazing how the years whiz by, and you don't even notice because you're busy doing this and that. Shirley and I have two thriving boys and a little daughter with a ponytail and skinned knees. As anybody can guess, she's the apple of my eye. And I have a beautiful wife. As a kid Shirley was pert; now she's beautiful. Ask anyone. Whatever remarks the neighbors make I don't hear. I have a nice Cape Cod, with a good rate on the mortgage.

When they close the *Newsletter* down and I lose my job, I'll look around. I like my job. I know a writer has no real control over a story, only over some of the words, but I'll find something else. I'm pretty tight with everybody in town.

Right now the town is excited. Charlie is home. He has already been to see me. He is sugar-haired now, with little blue eyes like a pervert's. I can only speculate what happened to him in prison.

"I've been in the brig, Sonny." Those were his first words, quick little chirps.

"I know, Charlie. I was happy to hear about your release."

A hint of ferocity enters his makeup. "You oughtn't to have let them take me away."

"I know, Charlie."

"You ought to have done something, Sonny."

My voice sags. "I know."

Then, with those tiny eyes, Charlie examines framed photographs of my children. The older boy has a wave in front and is a bit heavy in the face. The younger one has a cowlick that sticks out in back and, rather than making him look ridiculous, gives him the majestic air of a blue jay. Charlie focuses on my little daughter, who has mostly Shirley's looks and only faint traces of mine. I have to admit she was my favorite the moment she was born.

"She's a real honey," Charlie says.

He has settled himself in a furnished room near the Ioka, where he never misses a Saturday matinee. He takes his meals at Kurtz's Diner, after which he takes long walks, especially after supper. He and Chief Boitt have become close friends, and most people in town stop to chat with him or at least wave a sympathetic greeting. They don't know that Charlie has his eye on my daughter.

BANG BANG

Wyatt and Fay Eklund sipped drinks on the veranda of a small resort hotel on the Cape. Fay, lustrous and conspicuous in an open shirt over a brief bathing suit, drew covert glances from other tables, but she was used to that and would've been mildly dismayed had she sat unnoticed. Wyatt's attention was on the beach, where the lone figure of a man was following the surf. Wyatt abruptly rose from his chair. In yachting cap, royal-blue jersey, and white ducks, he had the stance and swagger of a reserve naval officer on active duty. "I think I know that guy," he said, shading his eyes.

Fay said, "How can you tell from here?"

He strode to a table occupied by an elderly couple, the Boyds, regular summer guests at the hotel, and snatched up Mr. Boyd's binoculars, training them on the man he thought he had recognized. Mr. Boyd, whose jowls wobbled his face, said, "Is that someone you know?"

"Could be. Could very well be."

Mrs. Boyd, her face dense with makeup, said, "You have a lovely wife."

Wyatt returned the binoculars and, with a knowing smile, rejoined Fay. "God damn," he said. "If that's who I think it is, he was one of my professors at Dartmouth. That was about ten years before he killed his wife."

Fay shuddered. "Why isn't he in prison?"

Wyatt sipped his martini while his free hand grazed his wife's knee. "Two mistrials. They let him go."

The Boyds were on their feet. Mrs. Boyd's permed hair was the yellowish pink of a tea rose. Mr. Boyd, a retired marketing executive for Nabisco's cookie and biscuit division, had protruding eyes that cast an air of aggression. He smiled at Fay and said to Wyatt, "Would you two like to dine with us this evening?"

"Can't," Wyatt said. "A friend of mine has shown up out of the blue."

"The fellow on the beach?"

The beach was now deserted. The sail of a distant boat looked like a gull's feather stuck in the sea. "That's the one."

Mrs. Boyd said, "Then bring him along, by all means"

"Not a good idea," Wyatt said. "He's a murderer."

Late afternoon, Wyatt let himself into the room. Fay was stretched out on the bed, her sprawled legs of superb shape and length. Huskiness gave her more value to the pound. He enjoyed gazing at her, as if she were prime stock. She opened her eyes.

"Did you find him?" she asked.

"He's not staying at the hotel. He's probably at a bed-and-breakfast. I mean, if he's anywhere."

"Why is it important you see him?"

"I never said it was."

Fay used an elbow to prop herself, auburn hair falling across her brow. "Why did he kill his wife?"

"The papers said she had a lover. Or a bunch of lovers. Or maybe somebody told me that. You hear a lot of stories."

"People love stories. Adds spice to their lives. Was he a good teacher?"

"He was a hard marker. Unfair, most people said. Shoved Pound and Joyce down our throats."

"He made you work."

"He was too damn tough," Wyatt said distractedly, as if feeding on the memory. He plunked himself down on the bed's edge and vaguely caressed the solidness of her calf. "His wife had red hair. Redder than yours."

"Mine's not all that red."

"That's what I mean."

Fay was curious. "Did you know her?"

"I talked to her once at a student-faculty luncheon." Wyatt cupped his wife's knee. "Her name was Rita. She was a beauty, like you."

Fay hiked beyond the bend of the beach to partial privacy, where she spread a towel on sand and shed her bikini top. Arms tight at her sides and legs stretched to the full, she lay in the midday sun and let the shadows of gulls glide over her. She enjoyed breezes on her body and salt air in her hair. As a child she had relished rain on her face and had run barefoot in the summer. In adolescence she had welcomed the boldness of her body and the mystery of her looks. She'd been a by-blow: she knew her mother, not her father.

She lifted her head when faint voices wafted in from a point where beach plum decorated dunes. At the margin of her vision she discerned Mr. Boyd in a breach of manners with his binoculars, which annoyed only a little. Mrs. Boyd led him away.

Evident from a half-mile away was a salt marsh's brackish smell, always tantalizing to her, and she wondered if it had winged the distance solely to intrigue her, to mark her as special. One of the few times she had not felt special was at a party with Wyatt and his friends. Listening to their reminiscences of boarding schools and European jaunts, she had felt doubly misbegotten. Another time was her first visit to Wyatt's family home south of Boston. His father, notably patrician, spoke in an easy voice that suggested the finer things in life, his mother was a preserved length of perfect manners and charm, and his sister had dazzling teeth that exaggerated an insincere smile.

Fay lay with the sun a lazy weight on her face. Eyes closed, she sensed a presence near the surf. Warily sitting up, she rapidly reattached her bikini top and made out the figure of the man glimpsed earlier, this time his face discernible, not at all what she had expected of a murderer.

"I didn't mean to intrude," he said from the short distance. His face was pleasant and agreeable, with distinct planes and a dry exactitude significant enough to be remembered.

"But here you are," she said. His graying hair seemed in the process of falling into place. Dressed in T-shirt and khaki shorts, he cut a reasonable figure. Suddenly he started to move on. "Please," she said, rising. "Wait up." With a leap and a skip, long legs flashing, she joined him and fell in step. Following the surf, they left tracks on a long wet carpet of sand. Waves rousting pebbles spoke a language she strained to comprehend. "My name's Fay. What's yours?"

His glance was oblique. "Manning."

"I understand you taught at Dartmouth. My husband was in one of your classes. Wyatt Eklund."

Manning shook his head. "Doesn't ring a bell."

"I'm sure you'd remember him if you saw him. Tall, exceedingly handsome. He wanted to be a writer, then a painter, but neither worked out."

"Some artists fail to defy gravity. Words, colors fall flat. Your husband could do what I did and teach." Manning shifted his eyes to the orderly arrival of waves, pebbles chattering, the wash ruffling the sand's edge. "So what does he do now?"

"He doesn't have to do anything. He comes from money."

They slowed their step and stopped. A whale-watching boat was plowing a path in from deep waters. Manning placed his face in a breeze while Fay wondered whether his murdered wife terrorized his dreams.

"He's been looking for you," Fay said. "He'd like you to dine with us at the hotel."

"I think not," Manning said, without explanation. His gaze trailed a gull shaving the surf.

"Wyatt will be disappointed."

"Then don't tell him you've seen me."

"That would be a sin of omission."

"Many sins are."

Fay found herself looking into calm eyes that divulged nothing. The only other killer she knew was Ray Hughson from her hometown in upstate New York. A month on the police force, Ray had responded to a call from the public library, where an eccentric old woman, Hattie Bragg, was causing a ruckus. When Hattie threatened Ray with her cane, he drew his service revolver and shot her dead.

Manning said, "Why are you staring?"

"Am I? I'm sorry," Fay said, and they resumed walking, sidestepping washed-up weed and wading through a hollow of warmish tidal water. The whale-watching boat, surrounded by swooping and squawking gulls, was curving away. In a careful voice, Fay said, "Wyatt read about you in the papers."

"So you know about that," he said without inflection. They were walking now where the sand was stiff, like asphalt.

"Should I be afraid of you?"

"That's up to you."

The afternoon was wearing down, accepting shadows in the dunes, which made Fay leery of walking much farther from the hotel with him. He was a sealed document, contents unknown. "I'd better turn back now," she said.

"I'll keep going." Turning away, he slowly glanced back. "What's your husband's name again?"

"Wyatt. Wyatt Ecklund."

"Wanted to be a writer, did he?"

"For a while."

"Couldn't have shown a great deal of promise. I'd have remembered."

The Eklunds dined with the Boyds after all. From a veranda table they could hear the tide swishing in. Fay wore a ribbon in her hair and a clinging dress, and Wyatt was spiffy in a blazer and a white shirt open at the neck. In Fay's eye the Boyds looked make-believe. She saw only the jowly dance of Mr. Boyd and the tea-rose hair of his wife, both baby-like in lobster bibs.

"You were joking, of course," Mrs. Boyd said, and Wyatt, consuming baked stuffed sole, shook his head.

"Who'd he kill?" Mr. Boyd asked and, with authority, cracked a lobster claw.

"His wife," Wyatt replied. "And got away with it."

The Boyds were depositing broken shells on a platter, which glittered like a bed of live embers. Fay imagined the glowing coals of hell and said, "His poor soul."

Mr. Boyd wiped the melt of butter from his mouth. "Why'd he do it?"

"Story I heard is his wife humiliated him," Wyatt said nonchalantly. "Her tastes ran sideways."

The steward, a corkscrew curl gracing his brow, fished up bubbly from the bucket, ice scaling off the bottle, and refilled glasses. Mrs. Boyd, rousted that afternoon from a dream in which a naked man had played a part, was intrigued. "What does that mean, sideways?" she asked as the steward moved off smartly.

Mr. Boyd, who had an aptitude for trigonometry, envisioned three-somes. "Use your imagination, dear."

"Women," Wyatt explained. "She liked other women."

Mrs. Boyd was further intrigued. "How did he kill her?"

"Bang bang," Wyatt said.

Fay, shuddering, deliberately shifted her gaze to another table, where young honeymooners clinked glasses in a toast. Fay saw traces of herself in the young woman and a bit of Wyatt in the man and wondered whether one would eventually kill the other for whatever the reason, be it selfish, silly, or senseless. Almost didn't matter.

The Boyds were scavenging the last of their lobsters. His teeth cracking a feeler, Mr. Boyd sucked out a thread of flesh. Mrs. Boyd said, "You don't often get away with murder. Or do you?"

Wyatt shook his head. "He was lucky."

"He must've been desperate," Mrs. Boyd mused over her champagne. "Maybe his wife taunted him with her misbehavior, drove him to violence, made him an animal."

"A crazy man needs no reasons for what he does," Wyatt said.

Fay came to attention. "Are you saying he's crazy?"

"He can't be right, can he?"

Mr. Boyd couldn't repress a belch. He had eaten too much, which didn't deter him from studying the dessert menu with his wife. Simultaneously they decided on peach shortcake. Fay and Wyatt ordered liqueurs, which arrived promptly.

"Pity you couldn't find him," Mrs. Boyd said. "It would have been exciting to meet him."

Wyatt laughed. "He was a professor of mine. You'd probably find him a crashing bore. Show me an academic who isn't."

"There's mystery in all of us," Fay said.

"What's your take on the fellow?" Mr. Boyd asked her.

Wyatt answered for her, a habit of his. "She's never met him."

The four of them rode the elevator to the third floor, where the Boyds vanished into their room and the Eklunds into theirs. Fay yanked the ribbon from her hair, and Wyatt lifted her dress, her underpants little more than a label to be peeled away. "It must be the salt air," he murmured.

"Or the champagne," Fay said.

He always entered her with a sense of triumph, as if he were a warrior and she the spoils, their bed a field of battle. Invariably lust pulled his face out of shape, which had once mesmerized her and now merely disconcerted her. Eventually he rolled away and, as usual, fell into a thick sleep. She was wide awake.

The moon glazed the beach. Carrying her sandals in one hand, she tramped barefoot over wet sand and salted her face in the ocean air. Mist swirled over the surf, which had lost its force and was retreating like winter slush pushed back by a plow. "I knew you'd be here," she said to the figure at the surf's edge. Moonlight glanced off the planes of Manning's face, and shadows nuanced it. Her imagination fed on him. "Did you really kill your wife?"

He glanced sideways at her. "I've never denied it."

She wondered whether he had suffered a psychotic episode. A deed done in the high heat of the moment, for which he was not held liable. They commenced walking together, the beach a river of pearly light. She dropped a sandal and didn't bother to pick it up. "Your wife had red hair. Like mine?"

"No. Real red."

"That's what Wyatt said."

In the moonlight gray touches at his temples looked powdered, endowing him with the air of a stage actor. Farther down the beach two couples were taking late-night strolls. Short-sighted, Fay glimpsed only their patterns. Manning spoke abruptly in a near toneless voice, surprising her. "Do you and your husband love each other? I mean, do you love each other very much?"

She liked to be truthful. About everything. "Just normal. Like most people."

"Then neither of you will do the unthinkable."

She didn't ask for an explanation. She didn't want one. Or need one. Was his wife, she wondered, the single rare moment in his life? She let the salt air ripple against her face. "Was she beautiful?"

"Rita was flamboyant. And a free spirit, which generated lots of stories about her, some half true, most false."

They slowed their pace. The only sound reaching Fay was the slushing of the retreating surf. "I have another question," she said. "Where do the gulls go at night?"

"Nowhere. They simply disappear and reappear in the morning." Looking off, Manning spoke from his chest, as if unloading it. "It's never easy to kill somebody, you know, even if that person is dying and suffering terribly. Rita wanted it to be fast. But my hand shook. God help me, I had to shoot twice."

Without warning, the faces of the strolling couples blossomed into view, their voices audible. Fay recognized the twosome, young and attractive, who had clinked glasses in a honeymoon toast. Neither, so far, had killed the other. Manning stepped away before anyone came face to face.

"It's late," he murmured.

Watching him move off in full stride, she called after him. "I'm not afraid of you."

Dangling a single sandal, Fay entered the lobby, nodded to the night clerk, and rode the elevator to the third floor, where she noticed that the door of the Boyds' room was open. Peering out, Mrs. Boyd drew her in with a frantic gesture. Without makeup, the elderly woman's face resembled fabric. Mr. Boyd lay silent and still in bed, eyes shuttered, covers drawn to his jowls.

"He's not well, but he won't let me call a doctor. It's his heart. Not good. Not good at all."

"I didn't know," Fay said contritely, as if she should've guessed. She had seen him put away food.

Mrs. Boyd seemed stuck in a spell. "I always do what he says, but I don't want to lose him."

Fay regularly deferred to Wyatt on all matters, overriding the fact that she had been president of her class at her community college, no grade lower than A-minus on her blue examination books, whereas Wyatt had finished at the bottom of his class and may not have even graduated, at least not properly. "Would you like me to call a doctor?"

"I don't know, dear. I've been so sheltered. My first husband pampered me and never told me anything, not even when he knew he was dying. He didn't want to upset me."

Staring absently at the weave of Mrs. Boyd's face, Fay chided herself for comparing her associate degree with whatever degree Wyatt did or did not receive and for pitting her little college against a hallowed institution like Dartmouth. Marrying her, Wyatt had plucked her out of working-class obscurity and given her the prestige of the Eklund name. "Tell me what you want me to do, Mrs. Boyd."

"I don't know. I've never been good at these things. Did you lose a sandal?" Mr. Boyd's breathing turned crooked, and both women turned sharply. Mrs. Boyd shivered. "I was young when my first husband died. I wouldn't hold his hand because I was afraid he'd take me with him. Things like that you never forgive yourself for."

Eyes open, Mr. Boyd uttered a sound that startled both women. His Adam's apple looked like blockage trying to break free. His eyes sought Fay and subjected her to a thyroidal stare.

"He wants water!" Mrs. Boyd cried, and Fay, with a start, poured bottled water into a glass. As Mrs. Boyd lifted her husband's head, he opened his mouth like a baby bird. "You do it," Mrs. Boyd ordered, and Fay fitted the glass between Mr. Boyd's lips as something infant-like took over his face. As he gurgled, his hand crept out of the covers and patted the bed. "He wants you to sit there," Mrs. Boyd said. "Could you do that for him?" Fay paused for a tight moment and then made a place for herself beside him, where she felt more a priestess than a nurse. "Maybe you could stay a few minutes, dear. And could you hold his hand?"

"Absolutely not. You should hold his hand, not I."

"It's yours he wants, dear."

Mr. Boyd mumbled something through a distorted smile, as if his face were in some sort of death grip, but then, his smile straightening, he entertained himself with a fortissimo of farts. Mrs. Boyd shot him a homicidal look that left Fay with scant doubt that, given hammer and knife, Mrs. Boyd was capable of shattering her husband's skull and slashing his throat.

Fay was on her feet.

Mrs. Boyd said, "You did wonders for him, dear."

Fay slipped out of bed after Wyatt left for a day of golf. Room service was prompt. She relished her first cup of coffee. She enjoyed skin-
ning a navel orange, the strong scent of the peels lingering in her nails.
Before showering, she struck poses in the mirror. Wyatt's sister had had
surgery to remove belly fat. Fay had an honest body, with a depilated
private area that made her feel like a child. From the window, the ocean
was rivetingly blue, drawing her to it.

Her face wrapped in sunglasses, she carried a nylon tote bag and a
towel down to the beach. A bevy of women occupied a shelf of sand
near the tideline while their squirrely children splashed in a tidal pool
in view of a lifeguard, who was a prince on a perch, sun block on his
nose. Fay hiked to the privacy around the bend, where she spread the
towel, undid her top, and oiled herself against the onslaught of a sun
edging toward its height. Legs crossed at the ankles, eyes closed under
blue-black lenses, she waited. She gave Manning an hour, though fifteen minutes was enough. Without opening her eyes, she said, "I knew
you'd come."

"You take chances."

She opened an eye as he dropped down beside her and stared at the
surf. "Does a bare bosom embarrass you?" she asked.

"Depends."

Sitting up smartly, she hunched her shoulders, embraced her knees,
and shielded herself. "I used to model, eight dollars an hour. That's
where I met Wyatt. Love at first sight, I guess. I was nude."

"Nudity has its own finery."

"Wyatt likes to show me off, picks out my clothes, my shoes. We've
been married only a few years, though we lived together before that."
She stopped herself. "Why am I telling you these things?"

"Some things don't need a reason."

Fay fished a snapshot from the tote bag and, while handing it over,
felt she was almost near enough to the shell of his ear to hear the roar
of his brain. "Now do you remember?"

Manning viewed the favorable features of Wyatt Eklund. Nothing
seemed to click, and his teeth shone in a smile that didn't last. "Sorry.
I've blanked out a lot of things."

Fay reclaimed the picture and deftly restored her top. The front of

Manning's hair tended to flop, and she watched him shrug it back. "Do you have children?" she asked, and he shook his head. "Wyatt and I have none. His decision and, I suppose, mine." Sensing he wasn't listening, she scrutinized the lines in his brow but failed to get a reading.

"Last night on the beach," he said suddenly and softly, "I was thinking of ending it, but you came along and brightened things up."

His words were a gentle assault on her sensibilities, for it was possible he was lying. Wyatt told lies all the time, and back in high school Ray Hughson had told her stories to get his way. She said, "You wanted to end it? That would be giving up."

"Dying need not be giving up. It could simply be a cease-fire."

"Do you believe that?"

"I don't know what I believe. At the moment I'm just throwing out words." A breeze off the ocean washed over them. A few friendly clouds roamed the vivid sky. "I'm leaving tomorrow," he said. "It's doubtful we'll meet again. Probably best we don't."

Fay felt a twinge, a longing to know more about him. The little she did know was already locked into a memory any stray breath of salt air would stir. She knew that as surely as she knew that every hello carries the inevitability of a good-by. A shadow fell across her. He was on his feet and poised to leave without a word. She sat up. "People shouldn't just walk off," she said. "They should part in a ceremonial way."

Without hesitation, he squatted in front of her. His face loomed. "The past is real. I'm not sure what I'm doing now is." He kissed her cheek, firmly, meaningfully, as if she were special, perhaps even a princess. As he rose, she gazed up with quiet eyes. Nothing to be said. Then he was gone, his absence more palpable than his presence.

Fay shared a table on the veranda with Mrs. Boyd. A waiter served them iced tea. "Goodness knows where my husband is," Mrs. Boyd said. "He wandered off with those binoculars of his and probably got lost. I sometimes think I should pin a tracking device on him."

Fay was smoking a cigarette, the first she'd had in months. She said, "You used me."

Mrs. Boyd wore a sun visor over her eyes. "Whatever do you mean, dear?"

"He wasn't dying."

Mrs. Boyd tasted her tea. "He was sick, you saw that."

"He's a pig. He overstuffed himself at dinner."

"He's an old man, dear. His joys are few."

Fay exhaled a great deal of smoke. "You shouldn't have asked me to sit on the bed, and you certainly shouldn't have asked me to hold his hand."

"It pleased him."

"And cheapened me."

Mrs. Boyd almost laughed. "You're overvaluing yourself, dear, but no matter. And no harm done. We're all silly at times, aren't we?"

Suddenly it became clear to Fay that in marriage Mrs. Boyd was meat and potatoes while naïve women like herself, surrendering their souls at the altar, were little treats, frosted cake, sips of punch.

Mrs. Boyd finished her iced tea. "I really should look for him. I never know where those binoculars are going to take him." Fay crushed out her cigarette, and Mrs. Boyd rose with effort from her chair. "I envy you, dear. My first husband was handsome in his day, but nowhere near as handsome as your husband. You're a lucky woman." Mrs. Boyd paused. "That's what I don't understand."

"Excuse me?" Fay said. "What don't you understand?"

Mrs. Boyd applied a smoothing hand to her tea-rose hair.

"Your friend on the beach. My husband said you made a charming couple."

"Really." Fay lit her second cigarette. "Then maybe you should pass that on to Wyatt. I'm sure his ears would perk up."

A false look of alarm flashed across Mrs. Boyd's face. "I'd never do that, dear. We women have to stick together." She winked. "Otherwise where would we be?"

After dinner the Eklunds went to an ocean-front bar, quite crowded, quite noisy. From their little table, where they were sipping Pinot Noir, Fay spotted him first. He was by himself at the bar, wedged in, jostled by strangers, smiling now and then in an odd way, as if his face were sore. Then Wyatt saw him and, rising, said, "No doubt about it. It's him."

Fay watched Wyatt snake his way through the crowd and approach Manning. She craved a cigarette, but there was no ashtray, no smoking. Crossing her thighs, the left over the other, she watched the two men shake hands, Wyatt the aggressor, Wyatt in charge, his posture martial. Then, weeding this way and that, his smile broad, Wyatt ushered Manning toward her and appropriated a chair for him. Fay immediately unclenched her thighs to make room, but there was little to spare. Knees bumped.

"He remembered me right away," Wyatt said with satisfaction. "I knew he would. Professor, meet my wife, Fay."

She and Manning smiled politely at each other, as if their meetings on the beach had never taken place, as if he had never placed a kiss on her sun-hot cheek.

Wyatt said, "I had the professor for Modern Lit. Joyce, Pound, Proust, those guys. The heavy hitters, he called them."

Her face an oval of feigned indifference, Fay remembered the kiss. It was poetic.

Wyatt's voice deepened. "You didn't give me a very good grade, Professor. In fact, you flunked me."

"Did I? I don't remember."

"You accused me of plagiarizing."

Manning had brought his tankard of beer from the bar, half gone, some in spillage on the way. "Yes, now I do remember. You nearly didn't graduate. A hearing was necessary. Your father came with a lawyer."

"I had my own heavy hitters."

Fay tried not to look at Manning. Their knees were unavoidably touching, steering her mind into places it shouldn't go. She stole a look at him in the event his face was giving out secrets. It wasn't. Not a one.

Wyatt said, "I used to watch your wife crossing the Green. We all had eyes for her."

"That's understandable. My wife was beautiful."

"Red hair. You couldn't miss her. We all felt sorry for you. We knew what was going on."

Fay's knee pressed decisively against Manning's in the hope of conveying a feeling she was sure was valid, that a man and a woman need each other if only for balance. She wanted it known that her father, her uncles, the spear side of her family, were weaklings. The women were warriors. She was worthy, she wanted to tell him, but he was speaking to her husband.

"If you don't mind, Mr. Eklund, I won't respond to that."

She wanted to tell him that her husband had wanted to be a great painter like Matisse, who was not much of a man. Matisse turned his back on his wife and children and sought safety in the unoccupied zone during the Nazi occupation. His wife worked for the Resistance, and so did one of his daughters. They were warriors.

"I may have cheated on an exam," Wyatt said, "but I never killed my wife. As you can see, she's sitting here alive and well."

"You're absolutely right, on all counts." Manning raised his tankard, drained what little remained. Fay felt his knee slip away. "Well, I must be going." She wanted to reach for his hand and hold him in place, but he was already on his feet and glancing down at Wyatt and then shifting his eyes to her. Her heart sank. He was viewing her as if she were a curiosity, nothing more.

"Not driving you away, are we?" Wyatt said.

Fay gazed up at Manning. He said, "A pleasure meeting you, Mrs. Eklund."

They watched him leave. With a smile of satisfaction, Wyatt said, "I've waited a long time to get back at that son of a bitch."

Wyatt was asleep as soon as his head hit the pillow. Fay, who knew he would be, went down to the beach, stood on a moonlit spit of sand, and let the ocean encroach on her. Waves broke nearer and nearer. Seawater rushed over her bare feet, chilling them. She hiked her dress when it splashed her knees, and when it threatened her thighs she stiffened, as if a cold claw were reaching up there, unkind, unloving. She retreated to dry land. Had there been any hope of Manning's showing up, she'd have sat on the sand, till dawn if necessary.

The night clerk noted her return with a nod and her bare feet with a smile, her pumps left behind, perhaps washed away like her abandoned sandal. A growing fatigue weighted her legs as she rode the elevator and hampered her stride when she stepped out. The door to the Boyd's room was half open, which didn't surprise her. Mrs. Boyd was in a chair by the bed.

Fay spoke softly, with only a modicum of irony. "Another bad night for him, Mrs. Boyd?"

"This time I may lose him."

Curiosity carried Fay into the room. Mr. Boyd lay with his mouth open as if to draw a last breath, his eyes near-zeroes. His face seemed to lack not only meaning but identity as well. Frozen in her chair, Mrs. Boyd spoke mechanically.

"I'm afraid to move. I want the chance to say goodbye."

Fay gradually became aware of unmistakable sounds seeping through the wall. The honeymooners were exerting themselves. She and Wyatt had gone to Florence on their honeymoon. That was when he still wanted to be a painter, a noted one, and was sure he would be. She kept her doubts to herself.

"We've had a good life," Mrs. Boyd said. "I don't know what I'll do without him."

Wyatt took her to the Uffizi to see Titian's *Venus of Urbino*, Venus lying languidly in the altogether, roses in one hand, her groin in the other. In their hotel room, at his urging, she reconstructed the pose so that he could sketch her for a painting he had in mind, one that would exalt and immortalize them both. Instead he hovered over her with a look in his eye, and the sketch was never done. It was a game he liked to play.

With vacant eyes, Mrs. Boyd said, "I have no children, none whatsoever. When I was young, a hysterectomy left me with an empty dish."

The honeymooners were at the height of their entertainment. Fay could almost feel the heat in their voices aswirl in her ear. The man's voice was pitched high like a boy's while the young woman's had gravel. Mrs. Boyd was oblivious of everything except the chill of impending loss and aloneness.

"Did he make a pig of himself again?" Fay asked.

"A little." Mrs. Boyd gripped her husband's hand as if to anchor him, as if he had a tentative foot in the spiritual world and might drift away. "I regret he and I have never really talked to each other. You know, back and forth, real close, like a couple should."

You don't know how to oink.

"Were you about to say something, dear?"

Fay shook her head. Mrs. Boyd squeezed her husband's hand, and surprising everyone, perhaps himself the most, Mr. Boyd squeezed back.

WIDE WORLD OF WAR

In high school the boy Mimi liked best was Jarvis Carr, who told her she had beautiful eyes. "One is glass," she said, flustering him, and he said, "Don't do that! I never know when you're joking." Mimi's eyes, dark and luminous, revealed only what she chose while Jarvis, burdened with sexual urges, hid nothing. Inside his father's old Buick her breasts were soft toys. OK, she thought, let him play. Which eventually got out of hand. How could it not? Her fault, not his.

"Now you've done it," her mother said. "Does Jarvis know?"

Fleeing her grasp was a full academic scholarship to Boston University. "I'll write him."

"Write him? For God's sake, *phone* him!" Jarvis, who had enlisted in the army after graduation, was undergoing basic training at Fort Benning in Georgia. Her mother, a widow, was worried. "Will he do the right thing?"

"Nothing's a given, Mom."

She traveled south by bus, into pine and clay country, coral snakes not a rarity. Jarvis Carr met her in Columbus, where a Methodist minister married them. She wore a flouncy blue dress, and Jarvis stood tall in a baggy uniform. The minister said, "God Bless." Mimi murmured, "God bless the child."

In a motel near the fort Jarvis kissed her ankles, shins, and knees and worked up to her belly, soon to become a globe of the world. A few months later he was gone, on his way into the heat and horror of Vietnam. The baby was an easy birth, the child's first good deed. Mimi named him Evan, after her father, who had died of a staph infection when she was five. Her mother said, "May he be half the man."

The squad torched huts and opened fire on fleeing families. Everybody was an enemy, an infidel. Sgt. Carney in the lead, the squad circumnavigated the dead and dying, a feast for flies, dogs in the waiting.

A woman whose clothes had been burnt from her body made sounds like gurgles from a flushed toilet. Here and there, still clinging to life, mothers and children issued a medley of soft sounds, lullabies of patience and understanding. Jarvis, uncertain whether he was seeing form or figment, the real or the surreal, felt absent from himself. Sgt. Carney had lowered his pants and was defecating. It looked as if his bottom were rotting. Jarvis raised his weapon and would have fired had someone not yelled, "Down!" From afar came an explosion too big for the human ear, and Jarvis dropped for cover, his brain vulnerable despite helmet and skull.

Weeks later he sought out the chaplain, whose face showed more contraries than harmonies. Jarvis told him he felt he'd been in touch with God but couldn't swear to it. "God's a loner," the chaplain said through congestion, "so don't count on anything." Jarvis sensed pathology in the chaplain's voice. "And be damn careful what you believe, soldier. The Good Book is full of tall tales. Jonah in the whale, Noah in the Ark. Get my drift?"

The crack in Jarvis's face was not necessarily a smile. "So much stuff I don't understand."

"You're on a need-to-know basis. Like all of us."

"All this killing seems sinful. Is it, sir?"

The chaplain blew his nose into a khaki handkerchief. "Now you're trespassing into theology, which is masturbation of the mind. Let's not go there." The chaplain blew his nose a second time and viewed the result. "What you don't understand is that man's first weapons were his hands. They made killing lusty."

"Sgt. Carney died from heroin too pure for human consumption. That's what I heard. He did it on purpose. I heard that too."

"Let's hope it made him happy."

Slung from Jarvis's shoulder was a fully loaded weapon, the safety off. The chaplain had no idea how close Jarvis came to using it. That night he wrote Mimi, *I might not make it.*

Mimi seldom watched television, never the news. War footage was ubiquitous, numbing. Instead she read as if still in school, high grades to be achieved, college still in the cards. And she listened to baby sounds that one day would turn into talk. *Evan has your cowlick and maybe your chin*, she wrote Jarvis. *My mother says the rest is me, but we'll see."* Her mother minded the baby weekdays while she worked the switchboard at the local newspaper and submitted stories to the women's page editor, Glendora Newall, whose masculine looks implied a compromise. Returning the stories, Glendora said, "You're not there yet, kid, but keep trying."

A dreamer at the switchboard, she scribbled ideas on scraps and concocted lists of books to read. Evenings, stinting on sleep, an ear keyed to the baby, she read Anais Nin's early diaries and later wrote a review. Glendora tossed it back. "You don't get it, do you? This is a suburban paper, not the *Paris Review*." Fighting a blush, Mimi took a call and plugged in a connection. Glendora hovered. "By the way, talk is I'm a dike. I'm not. Aren't you glad we got that out of the way?"

Mimi wrote about a mailman, Ozzie Dubovy, whose route was heavy on magazines, an overload for satchel and shoulder. A bachelor, Ozzie considered patrons his family and ran their errands, remembered their birthdays, and lent them money when they were hard up. He bought flowers for the ailing, visited them in nursing homes, went to their wakes. Some said he was gifted or cursed with simple greatness, a little fellow with a huge soul. A week from retirement Ozzie was found on the sidewalk beside the spillover from his weighted satchel, a victim of chest pains long ignored.

Copy in hand, Glendora said, "Now this shit I can use."

Pfc. Jarvis Carr lay for months in Landstuhl Army Hospital in Germany where a surgeon mined his body for shrapnel and a shrink tried to double as an exorcist. Months later they sent him home, half himself and half someone Mimi didn't know. She introduced him to Evan and watched father and son shy away from each other. Evan played with blocks and Jarvis drifted into moods, avoided looking for work, and spent inordinate hours at the VFW post, where his disability check covered his bar tab, all of which made Mimi wonder whether she'd ever been fully in love with him. Half maybe, at most. "Don't," she said. She did not like his touching her. His blinking bloodshot eyes were fire-flies in her face, his breath pure booze. Fearing another pregnancy, she pushed him away. "No more. Not till you wear something." He took her anyway. His right, he told her. His due, damn it! In heat, he radiated imbecility.

Abused, she said, "You ever do that again, I'll divorce you."

His face retracted to the bone, where it appeared deadly tired, features not entirely his. His voice was arid. "Have you ever cheated on me? If you have I'll have to kill you."

"What did you say?"

He left the bed, uncertain, unsteady, and went into the bathroom, where he swallowed a pill, then another for good measure. Returning, he said, "That was the booze talking. Wasn't me. I'm not like that." He slept, his snores a brutal language for whatever was happening in his head. Hours passed. Mimi was not really awake. Simply unasleep.

Her mother said, "You can always move in with me." Not an option. Her mother's apartment was smaller than her own and accommodated overfed indoor tabbies. She didn't want her child growing up with dander, litter boxes, and allergies.

Jarvis became a regular at the VFW, where he listened to war stories while never adding his. He knew the tales that rang true and those that didn't and preferred the false ones, comic book material, thrilling fictions that did the flag proud. He frequently gazed at the mirror behind the bar, as if keeping an eye on himself, ready to act if he got out of hand.

Jobs came and went. Wearing a roughcast Brinks uniform, he hauled money sacks into banks and supermarkets but was let go for firing his weapon at flying objects. *Friggin' pigeons!* He clerked at a convenience store until the weight of his moods oppressed customers. He joined a work crew paving roads for the city and soon suffered a severe sunburn. Mimi suggested he go back to school. Northern Essex Community College. Or Northeastern. Cords protruded from his neck. "Why would I want to do that? I've already been taught more than I can handle."

"Are you busy, Miss Newall?"

"For Christ's sake, call me Glendora."

"I don't know if you've noticed, but I write better than anyone else here. I'd like to go on staff."

"Sick of the switchboard, are we? We'll talk about it."

The managing editor wondered if she were ready. "Ready?" Glendora said. "The girl's a natural."

Glendora gave her a desk near hers and, along with regular assignments, a column to write. Over cafeteria coffee, Glendora lit a cigarette and said, "Lots of things you can write about. Women who wear their sour marriages on their faces, or maybe a piece about your husband. Vietnam vets. War's over. Does he ever talk about it?"

"He's full of privacies." Mimi spoke over a coffee cup, her lipstick on the rim. The cafeteria was a row of machines. "We married young."

"You made your bed. Doesn't mean you have to tuck it in." Glendora blew smoke. "I was married twice. First husband was horseshit, the second garbage. No kids by either, thank god. I was careful. You obviously weren't."

Mimi was letting her coffee go cold. "Tell me about Horseshit."

"He was a hitter. I hit back. He hit harder."

"And Garbage?"

"A degenerate. Enough said." Glendora crushed her cigarette out, then used the stub to pilot ashes to a corner of the ashtray. "Tell me about Jarvis."

"He has a hellhole in his head. I think it's where he lives. Doesn't trust shrinks, so he wants God to help him."

Glendora sighed. "Tell him God doesn't have a face, only a following."

Mimi's doing, Jarvis had a three-o'clock with Dr. Wall, whose office was in Boston. Crossing the Common, he sensed a call-to-arms, as if some historic bell were ringing. Entering the building, he saluted a uniformed man who may have been a doorman and nodded to a heavy woman who in a white winter coat looked like a polar bear. He rode the elevator, entered an office, then an inner one, where Dr. Wall awaited, his flowering bowtie frothing under two chins. VA credentials had accessed a printout of Jarvis's mental diagnosis, depression and anxiety boldfaced, paranoia probable. Jarvis fidgeted in an engulfing leather chair, and the doctor said, "What's upsetting you, Mr. Carr?"

Jarvis's mouth looked stitched. Then threads tore loose. "My son's turning six, and I still don't know him. He keeps his distance, I keep mine. Matter of trust. In Nam you trusted no one, except your buddies. Over there we were Biblical. We were God wreaking vengeance. But what do I know, Doc? I'm a loony."

"You sound bitter," Dr. Wall said quietly.

"I wasn't bitter, I wouldn't be human. But if I *wasn't* loony, I still wouldn't be right in the head. You understand what I'm saying?" Jarvis's smile was a rip in his face. "You believe in God, Doc? Give me the truth. No bullshit."

Dr. Wall flexed his stare. "I believe chimps and monkeys are our relatives. I don't know about hyenas, but probably. You seem to be asking the questions."

"That's because I never did. Someone told me something, I believed it. Someone waved a flag, I saluted it. By the way, I've been having these dumb dreams. I hear someone crying in the dark and gradually realize it's me. Scary, huh, Doc? How cracked am I?"

"How cracked is anyone? We're all different."

Jarvis slipped into an abstraction that put distance between him and the doctor's desk. Tears crept into his eyes. "There I go again."

Turning ten, Evan read *Huckleberry Finn*, *The Call of the Wild*, and *David Copperfield*, books his mother bought him. He read what his grandmother read, *Forever Amber*, and practically everything Frank Yerby wrote, which gave him soggy impressions of love and sex. On his own he read his mother's copy of *Heart of Darkness* and thought he understood it but wasn't sure. His mother said, "It'll catch up to you."

He wore Nikes, pedaled an old Schwinn, and played in Little League. His mother attended games when she could, his grandmother when his mother couldn't, and his father when he was sober. His father said, "Time we got to know each other." But his father didn't know where to start, and Evan didn't know how to help, which drove them deeper into themselves. His grandmother advised him not to be overly friendly with himself, a warning against masturbation, which flew over his head.

His closest friend was Mary Ann Rooney, a schoolmate with a temper and a crush on him that he was too shy to acknowledge. Once, in a fit of anger, she jabbed him with a No. 2 pencil and another time bit his finger, each assault requiring a nurse's attention. "Something's wrong with that Rooney girl," his grandmother said. His father said, "Don't ever show her your dinky, boy. She'll bite it off." His mother reacted instantly. "Cool it, Jarvis!"

Mary Ann, the youngest of six siblings, was blue-eyed and blond, with a small face and A's and B's on her report card. Walking to school, she splashed through standing water Evan avoided, she drew attention to a neighbor's dog when it cocked a hind leg, and gave a tug to cotton underpants with little life left in the elastic band. Nearing the school she hopscotched around a puddle. One of her sodden sneakers had a hole in the toe. "My mother says your father's an odd number and needs help."

Part of Evan's shirt was out. He tucked it in. "Odd number?"

"Like three, five, seven—you know."

"What kind of help did your mother say my father needs?"

Mary Ann yawned like a cat. "She didn't."

"I think I know." Evan squinted sideways at her. "Don't ever bite me again. I could get blood poisoning."

"Boys hit," she said. "Girls bite."

Responding in her column to a distraught reader, Mimi likened divorce to snipping a worm in half and creating two separate states of existence, each going its own way, one having little, if anything, to do with the other. Glendora said, "You've been thinking about it, haven't you?"

"For a decade," Mimi said grimly. "Had Jarvis been killed in Vietnam, memories would have stayed sweet. Now, God help me, things get on my nerves. Little things. I hate it when he eats sardines from the can."

"Horseshit used to do that."

"The way he tosses and turns at night."

"You think I enjoyed Horseshit? Dump him, for Christ's sake."

"I feel responsible."

"That's what women do. Get yourself a life, kid."

"I'm no longer a kid."

"All the more reason."

Mimi entered Dr. Wall's office with the same extreme dignity she bore when visiting her gynecologist and thanked the doctor for seeing her. Outside the window the weather was winter, but Dr. Wall's bowtie was a summer blossom. Laid out on his desk, his hands looked too delicate for a man. Mimi spoke calmly. "At times I don't think he knows me."

"He knows you all right, Mrs. Carr. The person he doesn't know is himself."

"Vietnam was ten years ago."

"Not for him. It's in his face every day."

Mimi sat stiffly, legs severely crossed, as if one canceled out the other. "Why are you staring?"

"Your husband claims you have a glass eye."

"Inside joke. When I was in high school I found life funny. Now it's merely a phenomenon."

"May I ask how you're doing?"

"I get terribly lonesome. Do you have a pill for that?"

Her words seemed to glance off Dr. Wall, who squinted through round rimless glasses. "I understand you missed out on college. Do you blame your husband?"

"I blame myself. I don't know what he'd do if I made him pack up and leave. His only friend is a fat man, a fellow vet and drinking buddy." She let several heartbeats pass. "I need to know, Doctor. Can he survive the shock of a divorce?"

"How can you truly get inside another person's head, Mrs. Carr? All you can do is make educated guesses."

"So you can't give me a straight answer, which is what I came for."

Dr. Wall adjusted his glasses. His eyes were two cents. "Ask the fat man."

Under an American flag hanging from a rafter, each carried a glass of beer from the bar toward a small table. He was laboriously fat, each wheezing step a major exertion, his movements sluglike. Slugs, Mimi knew from high school biology, move by muscle waves producing mucous. This fellow produced sweat. Seated, his bulk overlapping the chair, he blew foam off his beer and got some on his face. No eyes, just chinks. His lips were fatty morsels.

"In Nam I weighed normal, case you're wondering. I'm fighting flesh. Your husband's fighting himself."

"Sort of comes out to the same thing, doesn't it?" Mimi lifted her glass and sipped once, twice. The only other patrons were a few older men with meager heads of hair. "Is your name Checkers or Checker?"

"Singular, ma'am. Like myself."

Mimi worried about the chair collapsing under his bulk. She worried about Jarvis walking in and visualizing conspiracies. Armed, even unarmed, would he kill them both? "Were you and Jarvis in Vietnam together?"

"Different times, but we saw the same stuff, though he might've seen more."

"Does he talk about it?"

"Why would he want to?" Checker farted, as if he were alone, the world elsewhere.

"You're not a pig," Mimi said. "At least excuse yourself."

"Sorry, ma'am. 'Scuse me." He hadn't touched his beer. Now he quaffed half and swabbed his mouth with his hand. "We don't talk about it because people don't understand and wouldn't give a shit if they did. Holidays they pretend."

"Checker, you know Jarvis pretty well, don't you?"

"We share something is the most you can say."

"If I divorce him, will he hold up?"

Checker finished his beer. "Ask his shrink."

They sat down for what Jarvis considered serious talk, but first Mimi needed to know whether he'd been drinking. He shook his head, and she looked him in the eye.

"Swear?"

"Swear."

"Are you still going to AA?"

"It's not easy, all that religious stuff they throw at you. Jesus is the last person I trust."

"OK, Jarvis, I can understand that. What is it you want to talk about?"

He set his face. "Have you cheated on me, somebody at work maybe?"

"What if I said yes?"

"I would understand."

"Then let's leave it at that."

"Do you love me?"

"I'm doing my best."

They were high school seniors. Evan Carr occasionally smoked pot because Mary Ann Rooney did, and she read Conrad because he did. In a cloakroom they sneaked kisses and feels. At seventeen he was tall, lean, like his father, and she was so pretty she pained his eyes. "I love you," he said, and she said, "How do you know?" Then she surveyed the front of his pants for the protuberance she knew was there and said, "That's not always love."

She lived in a first-floor tenement vacant during the day. Her parents worked, her siblings were on their own. She and Evan had skipped school to be there. She lay on her bed. When he started to speak, his voice broke and couldn't mend itself. It was the first time he had seen a female naked. Her breasts appeared companionable, as if they relished each other's company. The butterfly tattoo near her navel was recent, the wedge of intimate hair was garnish. When he arched over her, she sensed a hesitation and guessed the reason. How sweet. "It's all right, Evan, you're not the first."

He was brought up short, the moment gone.

The next day in school she said, "Would it help if I say I'm sorry?" Then she reconsidered. "No, I'm not going to. When you grow up, let me know."

Later in the week, before history class, he apologized and drew a shrug. The senior prom loomed. "We're still on, aren't we?" She shook her head. She was going with someone else, Maxie Morrisette, a three-letter athlete with a scholarship to Michigan State. Evan murmured, "Was he the one?"

"None of your business."

"What happened to us, Mary Ann?"

"The world's not what you want it to be. It's what it is."

The prom came and went. He didn't go. Mary Ann went with Maxie Morrisette and another couple. After the prom, Maxie at the wheel of a Pontiac Trans Am, they sped away for the traditional dinner at a Route One restaurant but never made it. The car went airborne, the crash was horrific. The sole survivor was not Mary Ann.

Graduation was the third week of May, the ceremony held at the football stadium, the day mellow with the sweetness of the season and the nearness of summer. His father, uncomfortable in a seldom-worn suit, shook his hand, his mother embraced him, and his teary grandmother said, "I remember when your mother brought you home."

"Sometimes so do I," Evan said.

Addressing classmates, Maxie Morrisette said, "I'll never forgive myself."

Evan whispered, "Neither will I."

"Dumbest damn thing you could do," Jarvis said and began to cry, embarrassing himself and his son more.

"You did it," Evan said.

"Dumbest thing I ever did. Have you told your mother yet?"

Mimi took it stoically until the day she saw him in starched suntans and standing tall, thin, and straight like a hoe handle, his cap cocked to exhibit a live-forever attitude. It was his father all over again, the gods ready to slap him down. That evening, readying for bed, she said to Jarvis, "Make love to me tonight."

Jarvis drew a breath. "I'm a little out of practice."

"It'll come back."

George and Barbara occupied the White House when Iraq invaded Kuwait and the United States retaliated, other nations lending a hand.

Evan hoped to join the action, but the war was swiftly over. His father said, "He dodged the bullet."

Over lunch Glendora said, "Keep your socks on, kiddo. I'm getting married."

"Not to another Horseshit, I hope."

"No, and no more Garbage. This one's a secular Jew—no way could I marry a religious one, too close to a raving Baptist or a hardcore Catholic. He's a widower, lives in Manhattan. Met him on my last cruise."

"I'm floored," Mimi said.

"Knew you would be. I practically undressed for him, bared all my faults, and he wants me anyway. I even told him of a recent indiscretion. No, not with a man."

Mimi's eye fastened on Glendora's face. "You once said you weren't a dike."

"No one's a hundred percent this or that." Glendora scanned the menu critically, bottom lip sucked in. "Trying to drop a few pounds. By the way, I've recommended you for my job. Good luck, girl."

Bladder problems made the place smell like a urinal, and odors of incontinence added to it. "Jesus Christ, I've got to get out of here," Jarvis muttered but stayed the course to Room 202, where Checker lay, a diabetic deprived of lung power and lower extremities. Jarvis looked in on him. "It's me."

"Had to be you. No one else would come." From the corridor came a contest of coughing spells. Which one was worse? Checker spoke without breath. "Who gives a fuck?"

"What?"

"Nothing." Checker wiped sweat from the fat of his face. "In Nam we looked out for each other, didn't we? We were good buddies."

"We weren't there the same time."

"Must've been in spirit." Checker floated a smile. "To look at me you wouldn't believe I once had a girlfriend. She was a looker. Wish I had a picture."

Jarvis floated his own smile. "I had a girl too. I'm trying to win her back."

"I ever tell you I once saved your life?"

"No, you didn't."

"Remind me not to."

A month later Jarvis returned to the same admixture of odors, along with a new element, the unmistakable stench of insect spray. Room 202 was vacant. He caught the sleeve of an attendant. "I'm looking for the man who was in that room."

"Fat guy? He croaked."

Mimi lost her mother and grieved. At her job she progressed from Living Pages to City Desk to Editorial and caused a stir when she lauded Hillary for her cookie comment. She moved, with Jarvis, from the small apartment to a condo with wide windows that brought in a landscape of barbered shrubs and ornamental trees. Evan served his three years stateside, mostly on the west coast, and came home morose. His second week back he ran into Maxie Morrisette. "He should've gone to jail," he told his mother. "We both should've."

Mimi reached for his hand. "Don't do this to yourself."

"She'll never grow old, Mom. I will. She won't."

He visited Mary Ann's mother. A diary, which Mrs. Rooney had read, documented her daughter's final days. "You mustn't blame yourself, Evan. She didn't go to the prom with you because she wanted to teach you a lesson."

He bought an automobile, enrolled in a computer training school in Boston, worked evenings in a video rental store, met a young woman with red corkscrew curls and moved in with her, a third-floor walkup in a close-packed Somerville neighborhood where his car, along with many others, was a parasitic invasion. To add to his income, he joined the National Guard and hoped to earn a commission. The young woman, whose name was Rita, shook her curls.

"My soldier boy."

When he earned his commission, his father said, "If I were back in the army, I'd have to salute you."

Dr. Wall asked what was wrong, and Jarvis said he wasn't going any-where, simply spinning his wheels. "In the morning I wanted to leave my face in the mirror and be someone else, didn't matter who."

Dr. Wall's eyelids flickered. "How are you doing with your drinking?"

"I alternate. Good, then not good. What I am isn't what I want to be. You know what I mean?"

"Tell me."

"I don't know how. My wife says when I came back from Nam I was a dead thing pretending to be alive. She says now I'm doing better, breathing on my own. I don't believe her."

"Your wife's a smart lady."

"She's so smart, what's she doing with me?"

Mimi was home early and on the phone, a call from New York, Glen-dora on the line. "My secular Jew is going in for a triple bypass at Beth Israel." Her voice was at once harsh and hysterical. "Life isn't necessarily for the living, kid. The dead have comforts we don't."

"That's cheerful."

"We deserve better from our bodies."

Mimi stood at a wide window that brought forth a birdhouse hang-ing weatherworn and vacant from a maple. She wondered what man-ner of songbird had occupied it, what serenades had vibrated from the perch. Surely songbirds were happy. "I'll pray for him."

"That's a laugh."

"I believe in the energy."

Evan thought he might marry Rita and did. They eloped to New Hampshire and honeymooned in Vermont, after which Mimi and the bride had a serious talk over coffee at a Starbucks. "Evan's all I want, Mrs. Carr. I love him to pieces."

Mimi was sure she did and said rather hurriedly, "Listen close. The dance that's in all of us died early in my husband. I want Evan to have a better fate. Keep him moving to the music, Rita. That's all I ask."

Rita's red curls jiggled. "I'm not sure I understand."

"Nor do I, Rita. Not fully."

After 9/11 Mimi drafted an editorial. Iraq—make no mistake about it—would be on the Bush-Cheney agenda. Saddam Hussein and not Osama bin Ladin would be the prime target. Which displeased the managing editor, who said, "Who gave you a crystal ball? We're not running this shit. Mimi's face burned. "I wrote what thinking people already know," she said and turned away when he shrugged.

Victory was declared soon after the United States invaded Iraq, but the casualties, civilian and military, went on mounting. Within the year Evan's national guard regiment was pressed into service. Mimi took a pill to harness her head. Jarvis stood somber. "You realize he won't come back."

Mimi went white. "You did."

"Did I?"

In their third-floor walkup, Evan Carr's wife crawled into his side of the bed and slept there.

KATIE COURIC

When Montgomery's wife walked out on him, without warning, no note, nothing, she went from a real person to a semi-abstraction. The shape of her loomed but not the woman herself. He illuminated the whole house to lessen aloneness, all the time avoiding mirrors. He didn't want to pity his own image. In the master bedroom he viewed her denuded closet, imbibed her left-behind scents, and felt an odd sense of peace, as if he were dying. Which didn't prevent him from piercing the silence with the sound of her name.

CAROL!

A neighbor, Edith Flint, was blunt. "Why?" she asked, and he shrugged. "No idea." Which Edith, her face a wedge with a scarlet mouth, didn't buy for a second. "Do you even know where she is?" His eyes spoke for him. "Thought so," she said and gazed at him with a rush of sympathy. "Christ, you look ready for a religious order. Can't say you deserve this, Monty." She turned away, then spun back. "Or do you?"

Carol's brother was a man of leisure. Seniority had raised him in rank, well beyond his ability, which eventually caught up with him and forced him into a humiliating early retirement. Enthroned on his patio, he was lord of the realm, his weight straining the webbed seat of an aluminum chair. Singing grasshoppers owned a lawn buttoned with dandelions. Lilies planted by a previous owner had proliferated, roamed at will, and colonized in unlikely places, including a pebbly drainage ditch. Montgomery held back the sun with a hand while Ben lifted a loose Yankee face. "You're well rid of her, Monty—know what I'm saying?"

Montgomery glanced away. Ben was the elder sibling and the jealous one. Carol, blessed with the better brain, had been the family favorite. "Did she say where she was going?"

"Didn't say where, didn't say why." Ben rubbed his considerable chin. "Lot of things you don't know about my sister, but I don't tell tales. Stuff I could tell you, you don't want to know."

"You been drinking, Ben?"

"Not a drop. Face it, Monty, you never measured up, but don't let it get you. I never did either. We're second best."

A woman called through the screen of the back door. Sara without an *h*, younger than wives one and two and, according to Ben, marvelously barnyard in bed. The screen door opened, and Sara appeared in halter and shorts, her legs wands. "Can I get you boys anything?"

Ben whispered, "I adore her."

"I'm just leaving," Monty said. Having once glimpsed Sara in a thong, he wondered who besides Ben could worship someone with a tattoo on her bum, in Sara's case a butterfly.

Georgette Sims, who worked from an office in her home, served him coffee in a Red Sox mug. She was Carol's best friend, a cognitive psychologist and a survivor, victimized by a cancer that robbed her of a breast and a husband who left her after the surgery. She said, "Right or wrong, I'm on Carol's side. Women stick together. Or should."

Montgomery took a deliberate sip. The coffee was vanilla-flavored, which he could have done without. His voice was heavy with a question he hated asking. "Is she with anybody?"

"I'm not at liberty to say. I'm sorry, Monty."

He took a hard breath. "Is she safe?"

"Of course."

His mind felt too sore to think. "Could you ask her to call me?"

Georgette shook her head. She had boyish hair straying across her forehead and bracelets jangling on her left wrist. "She doesn't want to get into a conversation, Monty. I think you're losing her, so my advice is to pray. That is, if you believe in God?"

"Easy not to."

"If God's a *She*, I do. A *He*, I don't."

"You sound bitter."

"I'm bitter about everything. Carol has two tits, I have only one." Georgette, no secret, dealt with bitterness writ large in her clients but not in herself and once likened herself to a mechanic whose own automobile ran ragged. "You and Carol have a daughter, I have only me, not that I mind. Children never really excited me. How is Margie?"

His daughter was in Florence for a semester of Renaissance art. He had phoned her and, without asking, surmised that Carol had not been in touch and that in Margie's mind all was well with Mom and Dad. No need for him to belie the myth. He glanced at the wall clock and knew Georgette would soon have clients arriving. She was studying his face.

"We've both lost something, Monty. Who knows, maybe we'll end up in each other's arms. Wouldn't that be a blast?"

His faculty office was the size of a horse stall. Earlier in his career he'd taught history at a city university but failed to achieve tenure. In an endeavor to be democratic, he treated students, the serious and the lackadaisical, alike and perhaps shortchanged both. Now he taught at a community college where his classes were a mix of faces—chalk, ink, amber—and a colleague accused him of talking to himself and, out of courtesy, answering himself. With which he did not necessarily disagree, duly noted in a journal of stuff going on in his head. The journal lay open to current entries.

Self-deception is a felony too personal to prosecute.

Dreams in which your hidden self comes into play may shame you in the morning.

A summer student disputing a grade looked in on him. The boy was cross-eyed, his mismatched eyes dueling for position. "Can I come in, sir?"

Montgomery closed his journal. "You can, and you may."

Minutes later the student's grade rose from D to C-minus.

His journal reopened, he wrote: *In dreams, nothing is untrue or unreasonable.*

He was home, the nightly news on, when the phone rang. Carol's voice was arid, free of feeling. "I'm calling because I owe you that much."

His own voice splintered. "I miss you."

"Don't," she said, as if he were whining. He wasn't. He was merely stating fact, his heart a bird beating its wings. Was he speaking to her or to her doppelganger?

"Why, Carol? Why did you leave?"

"Why not?"

He knew she could manage on her own. She had family money, not a lot, but enough. "Is it another man?"

"If only it were that simple."

"Another woman?"

"Don't be silly." She paused. "Do you have company?"

"TV's on. Katie Couric." They looked a little alike, the two of them, both trim, sylphlike in their little dark dresses and tidy pantsuits. Like Carol, Couric probably looked pristine in white underwear. Even their voices were similar.

"Don't tell Margie. Not yet. Promise."

"What's going on, Carol? Tell me."

Too late. She was gone. Into the electronic ether.

Edith Flint appeared on the back doorstep bearing a covered dish and a fiery smile. "I can tell you're not eating right." Breezing by him, she placed the dish on the table. "Charlie loves my meat loaf." Her husband was an account executive in a company off Route 495 and sported a smooth face Montgomery judged too bland for purposeful thought. The heavy lipstick contorted her mouth. "No offense, Monty, but I don't know what Carol ever saw in you. I mean, you two aren't a fit, and she's probably been untrue all along. Never saw it coming, did you?" He wanted to brain her. "Truth is, Charlie and I are a loose fit. Good in some ways, bad in others." Her tone was conspiratorial, as if Charlie were not the only ingredient in her love life.

Montgomery looked down at the covered dish. "You don't need to do this, Edith."

"What are neighbors for?" She went up on her toes and splotched his cheek with her mouth. "Have to run, Monty. Charlie's waiting." She winked. "His night for fun."

Then she was gone. He lifted the lid off the meatloaf. Katie Couric was reporting on a record number of Gold Medals, musing whether Michael Phelps was a swimmer or a freak fish. Montgomery stopped short. Did Couric really say that? That was something Carol would come up with. He opened his journal. Edith Flint's mouth print still on his face, he added an entry.

Neighbors are nosy when their lives are little.

No answer at the front door. At the rear of the house he came upon his brother-in-law's wife stretched on a chaise, luxuriating in soft sunlight, no top to her bikini, zinc oxide snowcapping her nose. Gazing up at him through dark glasses, Sara grinned. "Guess what, I'm pregnant."

His eyes filled with speculation, for her sunstruck stomach was a dish. He said, "Congratulations."

"Ben doesn't know yet. You're the first."

"I'm honored, truly honored. Ben's not home?"

"Golf." She sat up, long arms and legs spidering the chaise. "I think I know why you're here, Monty. No, Carol hasn't been in touch." Suddenly on her feet, Sara tossed her weight from one endless leg to the other. "Hug me, Monty, I'm going to be happy as hell. I'm going to be a *mom!*"

They met for breakfast on the sunny terrace of the Bullard Inn. The waiter served Georgette scrambled eggs, bits of onion and chive mixed in, nothing for Montgomery except for the coffee he already had. He had arrived early. Georgette shook salt, her bracelets jangling. "That can be distracting, Georgette. Discordant."

"With some patients I take them off. Others I don't."

"I'm not a patient."

"What are you?"

"A friend."

"More like a relative of a friend." Georgette's smile was a fleeting display of big teeth in a narrow face. "When I was a child I had imaginary friends. Now I have only Carol. And, by extension, you." Her eyelids flickered. "I know you want answers, but I was her confidante. Same rules of privilege apply."

For a narrow moment Montgomery felt out of control and feared lifting his coffee cup. Nearby a woman was spearing chunks of melon. A boy in a white mess jacket was clearing a table. Life went on, though his didn't.

Georgette bit into toast, and Montgomery swallowed coffee he no longer wanted. Georgette said, "I was a good student, but Carol was stellar. Things came easy to her. Too easy. *You* came easy. You were a catch, a handsome young instructor—we all had crushes on you—but she may have expected a bigger fish." She paused abruptly. "Am I being cruel?"

"Only being yourself."

"Have I hurt you?"

"Feel free."

"Has Carol stopped loving you? Not my place to say, but maybe you could liken the situation to a chicken that for no obvious reason stops laying. Accept it for what it is. My best advice. "

Montgomery drew back in his chair. Too much was happening between his face and Georgette's, none of it nice. His coffee was going dead in the cup.

When the check came, Georgette picked it up. "My treat."

For supper he ate pizza provided by Domino and listened to news delivered by Katie Couric. "Twins," Katie reported, "are a brightness seen twice." Commercials swept Katie away. Back, she defined pornography as "sex without subtlety." Amazing. Katie's voice and Carol's words. Or vice versa. The two of them full of nervous energy. "In August," one of the two said, "armies of lilies suffer serious casualties."

"Sonofabitch," he said.

Edith Flint, without a ring or a knock, floated into view. "You're eating rubbish. I told you I'd feed you." She nibbled at pizza. "Charlie's in New York," she explained. She was wearing shorts, not her usual wear. "I have large thighs. Not my fault, I was born with them."

His phone rang, the one on the wall. "Excuse me." No one was on the line, only a few pips, as if he were disconnected from reality.

"Who was that? Carol? She's not coming back, you know. You're fooling yourself if you think she is."

He had the unsettling sensation that he was slipping back into a younger self. The Chevy in the driveway was the car he had bought used, his daughter had not yet started school, his wife loved him. "I need a favor, Edith. I need you to leave."

"Sure, Monty. Sure," as if she knew him better than he knew himself, as if she glimpsed something in him that was not quite honest and never would be. Alone, he mounted the stairs, entered the master bedroom, shucked his shoes. Windows open, muggy air swilled over him. He slept without knowing it and woke as if no time had passed, as if Edith Flint had not left.

"Don't act so surprised," she said. "You knew I'd be back."

Class over, he was stuffing books and papers into a satchel when a student approached, an intense young woman whose left cheek carried a blemish like a canceled postage stamp. "You said history is a catalog of horrors. Do you really believe that, Professor?"

"One war after another, Amy. But perhaps I was being dramatic."

"Did Hitler really happen?"

"Six million say he did." Montgomery closed up his satchel. "Viewed broadly, history is a vast receptacle into which myriad everyday people disappear forever."

"What does 'myriad' mean?"

"Many. More than many." He spoke as if true knowledge came from a sublime mind, not a conscious one. "Buddhists remind us that pleasure is brief and soon poisoned by pain."

"Are you a Buddhist, Professor?"

"I'm not anything, or least not anything in particular."

She spoke shyly. "You were in a dream of mine last night."

"I couldn't have been. I was in New York, just got back."

"Are you joking?"

He shook his head. "Simply putting myself in another man's shoes. Extremely uncomfortable, Amy."

Later he wrote in his journal.

Humanity is constructed so that there will always be a Herod, there will always be a Hitler. And there will always be Jews, whether they're Jewish or not.

Katie Couric smiled at him. Dipping into seafood salad from the supermarket, he smiled back. McCain's people were badmouthing Obama. Carol's response, guaranteed, would be: *McCain has gone from an authentic war hero to a total toad.* Ad hominem, without a doubt, and not something Katie would ever say. Katie was too professional for that. Carol, on the other hand, struck in wild bursts of self-certainty—no ifs, ands, or buts.

The phone rang.

More pips. His hand trembled. "Carol?"

"No, you fool. It's Edith."

Georgette saw him between clients and, bracelets chiming, said, "Don't push her, Monty. She is strong, but she's on the edge. She's making a turn, most I can say. OK?"

It wasn't. He wanted a window he could see through, a glimpse of a woman perhaps no longer whole. He rearranged his voice. "She's not a split personality or anything like that, is she?"

"Everybody's split." On her disheveled desk was an appointment pad to guide her day and a glass of milk to soothe her stomach. "You and I, Monty—Carol too—are at an age that's a damn uncomfortable fit. We're neither young nor old, with demons on the loose, the kind that chew on you, gnaw on your vitals, bite you in the ass, strip you down to your shortcomings, show you for what you are. Add to that, the country has turned criminally silly, arrogantly unjust. I hate what's going on. I watch CNN. Fox infuriates me, news filtered through Rupert Murdoch's feces. What do you watch? Anything?"

Should he confess? Katie. Only Katie. Peaches and cream. Sugar and

spice. The girl next door. "I don't watch much. Network, when I do."
He was studying Georgette's face. She was serious. She was passionate. "You and Carol are a lot alike."

"Of course. Why do you think we're such close friends? And you and
I, Monty, what are we?" Georgette leaned forward in her chair, placed
her mouth on the rim of her milk glass, and abruptly blew bubbles. She
looked up with a moustache and a smile. "Pretty childish, right? But
in the journey home, that's what we are again. Children."

His journal was open.

*Old-time Republicans, a dying breed, their blood blue, now cater to a rank
and file they loathe and detest. Their party is now the rabble.*

*High Noon: When Gary Cooper, exalting American individualism, stood
taller than John Wayne.*

He went looking for his brother-in-law and found him in the club-
house, a table near the bar, he and some golfing buddies discussing their
handicaps. Ben had a crest on his blazer and, from the sound of his
voice, snot in his nose. Allergies. Montgomery backed the car out without being seen and drove around the corner to Ben's house. Sara, wearing culottes, was hosing flowers, using her thumb to create a spray,
which she killed when she saw him.

"We haven't heard from Carol," she said. "Sorry."

"Would you tell me if you did?"

She tossed the hose aside and stood with long legs braced, attentive
to posture. "Of course I would, Monty. Why would I do otherwise?"

"I don't mean to be a nuisance. Thanks for putting up with me." He
feared he was becoming a bore, an imposition, and switched the subject. "What's Ben think of you becoming a mama?"

Her eyes drifted. "We've decided against it. Would get in the way of
things."

He wasn't surprised. Ben had children from his previous marriages
and he had debts, Carol an occasional lifesaver. Sara bent an elbow behind and gave a gentle rub below her back.

"My bum's sore. I had my tattoo removed. I didn't think it was fitting for a mom. But now I might replace it, the other cheek, not a butterfly this time. Any suggestions, Monty?"

His smile was tired. He could feel its weight, and he was sure she could feel the weight of hers. She stumbled toward him.

"Give me a hug, Monty. Keep me on my feet."

In his car, on the back of a sales receipt, he scribbled a note for his journal.

A moth is a butterfly deprived of color and coated with dust, as if something dreadful had happened to it.

The silence in the house threatened him. Shoes off, plodding in stocking feet, he raised windows to draw outside sounds and turned on the TV for faces and voices and got Katie Couric's. He imagined her in his arms, Carol's double, apparitional, ephemeral, which any crass commercial could preempt. Passing a wall mirror, he smiled, as if spotting a friend who had unexpectedly grown old. *Monty!* He was talking to himself.

The phone rang, and he snatched it up. No pips. His daughter calling from Florence but as if from the next room, her voice clear as a bell. "Everything OK between you and Mom?"

"Of course. Why wouldn't it be?"

"She called yesterday. Sounded different. You do too."

His mouth started shaping a thought he let dissolve. "What did she say?"

"It wasn't anything she said, Dad. It was the strain in her voice. She's not ill, is she?"

"No, Margie. She's fine. We're both fine." Not quite. His stomach was turbulent, his head encumbered by doubts. He viewed the back of his hand and imagined it mottled. A step to the left accessed another mirror, in which his eyes were open but his face was asleep.

"You'd tell me, Dad, if anything was wrong. You swear?"

"I swear."

Lying on the bed, he watched a *Law & Order*, an obvious repeat because Lennie Briscoe was still alive and kicking. Fixtures, old friends, were Sam Waterston and S. Epatha Merkerson, and he warmed to them while succumbing to sleep. Sleep soaked up whatever dreams he had until he woke. The smell of rain fell through the screens in the windows. A woman was in the room. Flashes from the TV highlighted her face and documented the rest of her, like a scene from an old black-and-white movie, a return performance, Edith in the lead role.

"Don't worry, Charlie's asleep. A jackhammer wouldn't wake him." Edith shed an old sweatshirt bearing the logo of Boston University. He almost expected tattoos to pop up, along with whistles and shouts. "I want everything, Monty. Same as your wife does. Life is short, wedded bliss is not."

The marriage bed wailed of Carol's absence. "You don't know what my wife wants."

"Sure I do. I'm a woman. Men are generic, except when they're not." She mounted him, breathed on his face. "Let me be the boss this time." Though he didn't intend to use excess force, she was off the bed, on her feet, her face a twist of contempt. "You bastard!" She pulled her sweatshirt back on and in the doorway, pivoted on bare heels. "What if I tell Charlie?"

Some of the rain reached him and moistened his face. Hers was a flared match he wanted to put out. "Good night, Edith. And tell Charlie whatever you want."

A light schedule, no students to see, no classes to teach till noon, so he slept late and ate a silly breakfast, salted radishes dipped in vinegar. The TV screen bustled with Regis Philbin talking through his nose as if fighting phlegm. Philbin was like a friend from long ago because he conjured up Phil Fumble from the funny pages, with Fritzi Ritz, Nancy, and Sluggo waiting in the wings. When the phone rang he instantly muted the TV. He didn't expect Carol on the line, but there she was, deep in his ear.

"How are you doing?" she asked.

Did she care? So much of herself consumed herself. "Where are you?"

"Everywhere."

Which was so like her. Aswirl. Hectic. Peripatetic. While mothering Margie she had flown from one thing to another, sometimes doing three or four things at once. She wrote poetry, taught Sunday school at the local Unitarian Church, and sang folk ballads in a Cambridge coffeehouse. She learned German and Italian, read Nietzsche, attempted *Finnegan's Wake*, waited on tables, peddled Avon, sold real estate. She walked. What she called walking, Montgomery called a hike. What she called a hike was the Appalachian Trail. She spent a summer at a religious colony, where she acquired a dazed and fatalistic look she soon shucked in favor of robust independent thinking.

"Come home, Carol."

"The furniture wouldn't remember me."

"You haven't been gone that long."

"How long, Monty? Forever?"

He shivered. Her absence was a weight on his well-being, a chill on his face, and suddenly he feared his face would metamorphose into a howl. For relief, he imagined himself fleeing, stretching his legs in Business Class, and flying to the moon, Katie Couric beside him.

"Katie," he whispered.

Carol said, "Excuse me?"

Georgette could see him because a client had canceled. "I should charge you," she said and sipped coffee from her Red Sox mug. The Sox, battling for a playoff position, were a game behind the miraculous Rays. Montgomery wasn't a fan. He said in a dry voice, "Sometimes I think I'm going nuts."

"Try not to. Amazing what we can do for ourselves when we put our minds to it."

"Are you taking me seriously?"

"When all hope is lost, take nothing seriously. That's what dying people do. To preserve their sanity."

He paled. "What you telling me, Georgette?"

"Giving you the benefit of my experience and insights. Carol isn't dying, nor am I, but we're in our forties, closer to fifty than we like to think. Men can get wrinkles, women can't. Women look into a future that's not that far away. Fear of dying, one day looking in the mirror and seeing nothing, not even your breath on the glass. Where are you, Georgette? No-fucking-where."

"Is that what Carol's afraid of?"

"It's what *I'm* afraid of. Carol can speak for herself."

"Have I lost her, Georgette? Have I lost her for good?"

"The answer's in *her* head, not mine. She wants to conquer the world, she wants to do everything, miss out on nothing. Failing, she frustrates herself on purpose. Now I'm telling you too much."

"Nothing I don't know. One more question, Georgette. How much of life is hearsay?"

"Every frigging bit of it."

He glimpsed her car in the driveway, heard her key in the door, watched the door open. They gazed at each other as if each had something to explain but the time wasn't right. Maybe tomorrow. Maybe never.

She said, "Who the hell is Katie?"

MRS. COMEAU

Her husband and her lover were the bookends of her daily life. They kept her standing, they kept her rational, and they kept her titles clear—wife, mother, mistress, dreamer. Sundays were for herself. While her husband took their son to church and later to visit his mother, she lounged in outsize pajamas that gave her a little-girl look. Over coffee she read the bulky *Times*, as much or as little of it as she wanted. She watched *Meet the Press*, or she didn't. When her cell phone chimed, she often didn't answer it. When she did, Liam the caller, she said, "Please, I told you not to." Liam wanted too much of her. Actually, all of her.

Dr. Wall had heard this before. "Are you taking your medication?"

Dr. Wall had a perfectly barbered ball of hair she imagined bouncing like a volleyball across the floor, against the wall, out the window. His gray eyes were pebbles plucked from a beach, and his bowtie looked spinnable. She said, "Can you help me or not?"

"The question is whether you can help yourself, Mrs. Comeau."

Her eyebrows shot up. "I'm paying for this?"

"If you feel you're not getting your money's worth, you should try elsewhere."

"Yes, I might do that."

But she didn't.

She had a lapsed driver's license and a run in her pantyhose, near the knee, when a policeman pulled her over for speeding and told her to step out of the car, please. She did so, with some humiliation. He asked if she had been drinking. No. She walked a straight line and did so without problem; in fact rather rhythmically. He asked if she knew how fast she'd been going, and she said, "Too fast. I'm sorry."

Standing smartly on long drawn-out legs, a knight taking pity on a lady, he issued no ticket, simply a verbal warning delivered with a slow look. He had a nice face, with an unobtrusive smile. No crypto-Nazi, this officer of the law, she was sure. "Thank you," she said and climbed back into her car. He looked in on her.

"Excuse me, Mrs. Comeau. Is your husband's name Gilbert?"

"Yes. Do you know him?"

"From high school. Not sure he'd remember me. He was a brain, I was a jock."

She had never considered Gilbert a brain. Knowledgeable about money maybe, little beyond. "What's your name, Officer?"

"Cassidy, ma'am."

"I'll be sure to tell him." She started up the car, a Volvo, and drove away through a glare of medication. "Cassidy," she said aloud. "I must remember that." But she didn't.

She was chauffeuring her son to a Cub Scout camp, which raised anxieties. Jeffrey was so smart he scared her and so vulnerable she wanted to cocoon him. He was nine, nearly ten, with the bill of his baseball cap facing back. She wanted to right it. He had his father's looks, her sensibilities. His father had determination, Jeffrey had dreams. "I'm not sure I want to go to this place, Mom, but I'm up for the challenge." She knew the words were for her benefit and patted his knee as yahoos on motorcycles roared by, skull and bones on their backs. Jeffrey counted cows in a field. "We almost there, Mom?"

Soon they were. The lakeside scene was a calendar page of pines etching the air, birds patterning the sky, and a hawk hanging overhead. Surface tension on the lake appeared musical. The camp director greeted them with a spread smile, his small trim moustache stretching almost to extinction, his rough-hewn legs sticking out of khaki shorts. His eyes fastened on Jeffrey. "You'll like it here, son."

Jeffrey gazed at a double row of cabins. "You don't know that, sir."

The camp director said, "Not to worry, Mrs. Comeau. The first day is always awkward."

"Jeffrey's not athletic, not at all. And he's a loner. His father wants him to be a joiner."

"All for one, one for all. That's the spirit here, Mrs. Comeau."

She saw his moustache as a mouse on the move when he spoke, smiled, squinted. Was he straight? He'd better be. She brushed fallen hair from Jeffrey's forehead. A crew cut had been recommended, which she had vetoed. He was signed up for the summer. "Try it for a while, baby, and if you can't stand it, call me. Promise?"

He promised.

She gave him two kisses. Springing up, she said to the camp director, "I'm leaving him in your safe hands." Which frightened her. She was at a stage where everything frightened her. Back in the Volvo, window lowered, she put a hand to her mouth and lobbed Jeffrey a final kiss.

Dr. Wall said, "Does your husband have a mistress?"

"Yes. Money. He caresses it." She took a deliberate breath. "His handwriting is small and cramped, practically illegible, which tells me he's anal. And he's putting on weight. I suspect the only exercise he gets is straining through constipation. How do you read him, Doctor?"

"I'm trying to read you, Mrs. Comeau. Do you dislike your husband?"

She went off on a flight of fancy, but snapped back. "Do I dislike my husband? I don't actively dislike anybody, Doctor." She farted delicately, as if shedding a feather. Nothing detectable, she was sure. "But Gilbert does get on my nerves. He's not a man, you see. He's currency." Dr. Wall's tracing a finger beneath his chin, near his bowtie distracted her, as did his eyes, pebbles pretending to see. "I suppose I could trade him in for a euro. Just a joke, Doctor."

"How about your friend? Liam, is it? Is Liam a man?"

"He's a writer who doesn't write, a grown man with an allowance from his mother. Essentially, he has great looks and little else. That says something about me, doesn't it, Doctor?" Dr. Wall jotted something on a legal pad and brought up the business of the bedroom. "Do we need to get into that?" she said.

"Not if you don't want to."

In terms of performance she rated her husband an unskilled laborer and Liam a finish carpenter, full service. One induced a quiver; the other an occasional quake. *Good show, Liam.* Liam always needed to know. Gilbert always thought himself grand.

"If you had to choose one or the other, who would it be?"

Liam had shoulders, her husband didn't. Liam was born in May, which put a bull in his birthday, and Gilbert was born in the dead of winter, a chill in his soul. Liam tanned in the summer, Gilbert burned. Or stayed eerily pale, as if deblooded. "I'm sorry, Doctor. What did you say?"

"If you had to choose."

"No choice necessary. Liam is a mild mistake. I'll end it eventually."

"And your husband, you'll keep him?"

"To do otherwise would disrupt my son's life. So I'm stuck, Doctor. Stuck."

Liam thought himself avant garde but wasn't. He was traditional, pre-dictable, his writing derivative. He was working on something. A story? A novel? An essay? She looked over his shoulder. Still on page three? That was where he'd been weeks ago. "I'm stuck," he said. "Can't get it to budge."

"Like constipation, Liam?"

"Yes." He pondered. "I might use that."

"We have to talk."

He knew what was coming. She'd been leading up to it for some time. "Don't do this to me."

"You knew it wouldn't last forever, Liam. I made that clear from the start."

He needed a hug, which she withheld, and a shave, which he could do himself. Or could he? He had arrived in the world out of wedlock, his mother a go-getter who had built a real estate business and rele-gated his upbringing to nannies.

"Is there someone else?" he asked.

She thought of Liam's mother as Miss Havisham in modern mode, her hair like fresh snow, season's first fall. Liam's hair was old gold, his face embalmed in remnants of youth. He was Pip, deprived, orphaned, peeking in from the outside, eyes trained on lovely Estella. "Don't whine, Liam. I'm not Estella."

"Who's that?"

"You're a writer. You should know." When she turned to leave, he gripped her wrist, hard, and twisted it. "Let go!"

He didn't.

A neighbor heard yelling, banging, threats, and called 911.

Responding officers were Peltinovich and Cassidy. Peltinovich, a young woman, new to the force, was at the wheel. Cassidy said, "You never know what you'll run into at these domestic things." They exited the cruiser, entered a tower of condominiums, and rode the elevator to the third floor. Peltinovich checked to make sure her pepper spray was handy. Cassidy patted his pistol, unfired in the line of duty. Its presence, along with his shield and his bearing, had been enough, so far. He caught sight of Peltinovich and himself in a mirror panel. "Two cute cops," he said.

"Speak for yourself," she said and threw him a look. "I'm not in awe of you."

"Good for you."

They emerged from the elevator. Peltinovich said, "I'll watch your back."

"Don't forget your own."

She flailed, freed her bruised wrist, shouted. She was dealing with a grown man's adolescent brain, raw ego, and primal needs. He wanted what he felt was his, all his, and he wanted it *now*. She heard her blouse rip under the arm. *Stop! Cease! Avast!* In a soprano voice she felt she was rehearsing an overwrought scene in a college play, her co-star emoting, venting, vaunting. He had a hand at her throat. She thrashed. *OK! OK!* Eventually reality sounded in the wings, a neighbor pounding the wall, outside voices crowding the corridor, and all at once an insistent banging of a nightstick on the door, a policeman's authoritative shout, putting bedlam in her ears.

Officers Cassidy and Peltinovich confronted Liam Fitzsimmons, whose speech was mostly spittle. Peltinovich stepped back. "Calm down, sir." Cassidy's eyes shot here and there. The bedroom door was half open, revealing a woman not yet adequately clothed but doing her hurried best. Wildflowers on her body were bruises. Each at once recalled the other. Her face flamed, but her voice was calm as it all came back, even his name. "Officer Cassidy?"

"Are you all right, Mrs. Comeau?"

"Quite all right. Thank you."

Liam, another matter, pulled open an end table's narrow drawer, and Peltinovich stiffened. "What are you doing, sir?" Pepper spray was no longer an option, for Liam was holding a gun. In the instant Cassidy produced his own weapon, a semi-automatic Beretta. Mrs. Comeau went white.

"Don't hurt him, Cassidy. It's just a toy."

"Put it down, sir."

"He's not himself, Cassidy. I gave him bad news, and he unwound. Liam, put that damn thing down!" Scarcely moving, Peltinovich knocked it from his hand, and it was indeed a toy. Plastic. Available at Walmart, Target, Toys "R" Us. Both officers shoved him into an armchair, as if he were a naughty child. Mrs. Comeau said, "He's harmless, just a writer. Writers are odd, Cassidy."

Cassidy's eyes gripped her. "Is he under the influence of anything?" She swore he wasn't, and Cassidy pondered the situation as Peltinovich looked on. "If we leave, is everything going to be all right here?"

"Absolutely," Mrs. Comeau said.

In the cruiser Cassidy complimented Peltinovich, told her what she did was pretty brave, and she said, "The more I looked at it, the more I knew it wasn't real. But we should've arrested him." Awaiting a response, getting none, Peltinovich started up the cruiser. "What was going on back there with you and the woman? Anything I should know?" Cassidy shook his head. Peltinovich ran the cruiser onto the road while spinning him a look. "How are we going to write this up?"

"I'll take care of it."

She dipped into poetry, Wallace Stevens, deeper stuff than she wanted, and that night in a dream the emperor of ice-cream asked if she wanted sprinkles. *Yes, please.* And, Jeffrey's age, she lofted her sugar cone bearing a scoop of vanilla. In the morning, after Gilbert was gone, she reached Jeffrey on his cell.

"You don't have to stick it out if you don't want to."

"Dad said there's no refund."

"Doesn't matter. I'll talk to him."

"Thanks, Mom."

She phoned Gilbert at his office. Exasperated, he said, "The boy has to learn!"

"Learn what, Gilbert?"

"Life."

"I'll make up the refund."

"That's not the point."

"Of course it is."

"We'll talk about it later."

That evening they watched cable news in bed, the sinking economy dominating the screen, stressing him, distorting his features, tiring his eyes. During a commercial she said casually, "Did you go to school with someone named Cassidy?"

"John Cassidy? Never liked him."

All of a sudden she felt tired, untidy, tremors in her face. "Why not?"

"Actually I hardly knew him. He was a jock. How do you know him?"

Lethargy lay heavy on her, like a man done with her but too lazy to shove off. "He stopped me for driving too fast. When I showed him my license he asked if I were married to you. Then he gave me only a warning."

Gilbert seemed pleased, his status recognized, his worth a factor, his world wider than he'd supposed. They watched the weather report, sunny tomorrow, temps in the seventies. Commercials returned with a vengeance, sports on tap. He killed the picture. Under the covers his foot brushed hers. When he moved to kiss her, she offered a pointed mouth, not a full one, the message clear.

"Not in the mood?"

"Not tonight, if you don't mind." He didn't.

He wanted time to negotiate the matter of a refund face-to-face with the camp director and told her to wait until the weekend to retrieve Jeffrey. She mentioned that the camp director had a silly moustache. He asked what that had to do with anything, and in a tone meant to sound serious she said, "Keep staring at it. It'll throw him off stride and give you a leg up." He abruptly rang off, a client on his other line. She phoned Jeffrey during his rest hour and told him she'd come for him on the weekend. "That OK, baby?"

"Mom, don't call me baby in front of the guys."

When the phone rang later, caller ID forecast a problem. She took a breath and said into the heated mouthpiece, "I'm telling you this for the final time, Liam. It's over. Over. Over. *Over!*"

His voice fell. "What'll I do?"

"What your mother would tell you. Be a big boy!"

Saturday. Gilbert wore a vested suit to convey presence, authority, command. With his weight gain, she thought he looked like a bale of nothing in particular. "We'll take the Volvo," she said, for she wanted to do the driving. His, overly observant, finicky, got on her nerves. Heading toward the highway, along the stretch where Officer Cassidy had stopped her for speeding, trees were brassy in the sun. Some seemed swollen. On the highway she picked up speed and passed an eighteen-wheeler. "Not so fast," Gilbert said.

An hour later the campsite burst upon them. Gilbert said, "What the hell!" Stepping out of the car, she said nothing. Dome lights whirled from three police cars, two local, the other state. A waiting ambulance sat empty, back doors winged open. Boys and grownups milled about. Absorbing the scent of pine and the smell of lake water, she steadied her stance, shoulders thrown back. The camp director appeared out of nowhere, face stricken, voice in shambles.

"No one saw him go under, Mrs. Comeau."

She wanted to dig his face with her nails for lies coming out of his mouth, for truths not told yet. Her voice was distant. "Does that mean no one saw him come up?"

The camp director went silent while she smiled through inner

calamity, the smile carrying the scent of her lipstick. When Gilbert
sought to help, she shook off his arm.

"How long has it been?" Dr. Wall asked, and she said, "Six months
this Saturday." She possessed a circular sense of time and believed that
aura and energy were eternal and that Jeffrey would eventually return
through some later woman's birth canal. How wonderful for that
woman! A gift from Nature. She said, "I may not need you anymore,"
and Dr. Wall said, "Are you sure?"

"Who's sure of anything, Doctor? I'm unsure whether Hell is fire or
ice. I've heard it both ways."

"Believe neither."

Saturday she entered the kitchen and found Gilbert there. They lived
in separate parts of the house now, the kitchen common ground.
Knives were racked like weapons of combat, hand-to-hand. The
chrome toaster distorted what it mirrored, at the moment her pale face.
Gilbert, poised over the morning paper with a pencil, enjoyed a cross-
word if it wasn't too demanding. "Morning," he said.

She looked at him as if he were nothing more than eyes, mouth, arms,
legs. In totality she saw a monster posing as a person. Her voice flat,
she said, "No three-piece suit?"

"What's that supposed to mean?"

She wasn't sure. Memories were uneven, and she was nerve-worn,
her sense of the absurd overactive. Her leg sliced out of her robe as she
confronted the coffeemaker. Her favorite cup was made in China. Sitting across from Gilbert, she reopened the subject of divorce. "I don't
want your money, only what's fair."

"Can we talk about this later?"

Sunday they went to the cemetery to view the newly installed tomb-
stone. The day overly bright, the greenery was wavy, inflated, hyper-
bolic, and the stone was marble, larger and taller than she'd expected,
the engraving keenly executed. She said, "Must've cost you a fortune."

"He deserves it." Gilbert glanced away for a second, more than a second. He seemed not to know where to put his eyes. "Can we salvage
our marriage? Please?"

"I don't like you, Gilbert. Nothing specific. It's more or less everything."

Terms agreed upon, divorce pending, house up for sale, she moved into a comfortable townhouse owned by Liam's mother, though she didn't know it at the time. Mrs. Fitzsimmons, passing by in an SUV, slowed, stopped, and lowered her window. "How do you like your place, Mrs. Comeau?"

She shaded her eyes. "I'm sorry, do we know each other?"

"You know perfectly well who I am, dear."

And, yes, she did. Knew the lady from pictures in the paper and a photograph in Liam's condo. Watched her emerge from the SUV, a confident creature in a tweed pantsuit a shade too tight, white hair spun into a headdress.

"I'm sorry about your loss, dear, but we all experience them. Liam's father died last week in his sleep. Liam never knew him. God sneaked in and blew out his candles. He probably prayed too much, and the Big Guy got sick of listening."

Mrs. Comeau was unsure whether to smile. She did without knowing it. Felt it on her face and sucked it away.

"Actually," Mrs. Fitzsimmons went on, "the poor man probably lacked the will to wake up. He was never strong, always floundering. Or is it *foundering*? Liam would know. I don't know what gives Liam the idea he's a writer, but it keeps him occupied. As you do—or did. Liam tells me everything when I have time to listen."

Suppressing an urge to slap the older woman's face, Mrs. Comeau retrieved mail from the box. Mrs. Fitzsimmons tugged at the hem of her jacket to stop it from riding up.

"You were rather hard on him, calling the police that way, but in the long run things worked out. The young policewoman with the Slavic name, she and Liam have become friends. That is hilarious. Along with loss, life is full of somersaults."

Mail in hand, Mrs. Comeau turned to leave, fast. "Nice meeting you, Mrs. Fitzsimmons."

Divorced, she felt undressed. All eyes were men who knew or guessed her situation—her financial advisor for one and for another the fellow in a faux-leather jacket who came to install venetian blinds. Subtly or bluntly, she let them know that what they were thinking was only in their dreams. Two days a week she volunteered at the YWCA, a relief, all the faces female, and on weekends she worked at the library, another safe place, until John Cassidy showed up. He was not in uniform, which was the reason she didn't readily recognize him.

"I'm sorry about everything," he said quietly.

Everything? Jeffery was everything. At the wake she had blindly received condolences, no images or voices registering. Weeks later, reviewing the visitor book, she saw Cassidy's bold signature. She still hadn't sent out thank-you notes. "Thank you," she said.

"How are things going?" he asked quietly.

She surprised herself with honesty. "One day at a time."

The book he wanted to borrow was a biography, *Kit Carson*. "Maybe sometime we could...." His voice dragged.

"Yes, Cassidy. Sometime."

"Not all the dreams are bad. Some are just unsettling."

"Relate one," Dr. Wall said.

"I'm in a deserted museum where statues of heroic figures and people in paintings gawk at me the way we gawk at them. Then suddenly I'm in the Sistine Chapel, and someone—God, I guess—shakes his finger at me."

"What's your worst dream?"

"The one I can't get out of my mind. I pat my son's head and tell him how wonderful that he'll never have to grow up, and he says, 'But I want to!'"

Watching her grip the arms of her chair, Dr. Wall said, "You have no guilt other than what you impose on yourself."

"What does that mean? Does it mean anything? Excuse me for saying this, but I understand most shrinks are full of shit."

"I suppose some of us are. How did you feel when you woke from that dream?"

"Nonexistent. The closest I've been to being dead but not yet buried."

"Is the new medication helping at all?"

"Sometimes it wads up my thoughts, gums them all together so I can't think. That's a help. Thank you, Doctor."

"You're angry."

"At the future, Doctor. I don't see one."

Dr. Wall puckered his lips as if to whistle and said, "Open your eyes, Mrs. Comeau. Open your damn eyes!"

They met at a little place near the library, ahead of the noon crowd. Cassidy had a bowl of crab bisque, she settled for coffee, strong, to her liking. "Tell me about yourself, Cassidy."

"Divorced. No children. Just as well, I guess. My ex-wife has remarried, lives in Connecticut."

His sumptuous use of shaving lotion slightly sickened her. At least it wasn't Old Spice, Gilbert's choice. For a few moments she circled what she wanted to say, then set down her coffee cup. "What's this I hear about Liam Fitzsimmons and your partner?"

"Ah, yes. Fitzsimmons got in touch with her, apologized, and charmed her in the process, especially when he told her he was a writer. She's a big reader. Stephen King, James Patterson."

"I'm not sure Liam's a real writer."

"He's close enough. She says she understands what you saw in him."

"Let's not discuss it."

"Good."

"I thought an affair would make me young again. I'd be starting over. What do you think of that logic, Cassidy?"

"I thought you didn't want to discuss it."

She lifted her coffee cup. "That's right. So drop it."

He finished his bisque with a smile she didn't find offensive. She imagined the years toughening his face while enriching it, adding wrinkles he'd welcome. He said, "You probably don't like sports, but in case you do I have tickets to a Celtics game."

"How exciting."

"Think about it."

He picked up the check. "One condition," she said on their way out. "Go easy on the aftershave."

They didn't go to a Celtics game. She lacked patience to watch abnormally tall men in droopy underwear gallop back and forth while someone in a striped shirt continually blew a whistle. "How about a chick flick?" she suggested facetiously, then said, "I'm not big on dating. Dinner now and then. Nothing fancy."

"What's wrong with fancy?" he said.

She liked his face, both boyish and manly, happy even when it lacked a smile. "I enjoy walking. Do you, Cassidy?"

"Call me John."

"I like Cassidy. And I'm vulnerable to sweet talk, so watch your mouth."

Wearing thick nubby sweaters, they walked around the city lake where Canada geese gathered as if for battle. A narrow path leading up a hill seemed to be hanging there, awaiting them. When winds deadened their words, each felt free to say anything. Could be tender, loving, outrageous, obscene. Could be anything, so long as the other didn't hear but might guess.

Their favorite restaurant was Italian. Their waiter, a recent arrival, wrote their orders on a tiny pad with excruciating care, as if practicing his penmanship and his English. Cassidy called him Joe. She called him Giuseppe. Over wine, as if aware of her sensibilities, he told her he had never fired his gun on duty, and she said, "I can't imagine you killing anybody."

Sometimes they ate in. She was a good cook, Cassidy was adequate. She preferred her place to his, for his was dreary, the oven unreliable. American history reigned in a bookcase built as if in a schoolboy shop class. In the cramped bathroom she repressed an urge to pour his aftershave down the sink. The shower stall revealed a trace of mold, which she bleached away.

"My place from now on. OK?"

In her living room, they read the Sunday papers. She plowed through the *Times*, he picked at the *Globe*, lingering with the sports pages. They watched *Meet the Press.* Politically she leaned to the left while he stood in the middle with a tendency to tilt one way or the other. Evenings, they watched *Desperate Housewives,* and afterward when she shed clothes, he found her at once vivid and mysterious, with any flaws fused into a perfect whole. She viewed herself in the mirror and saw nothing special. Later, time for him to leave, she said, "It would make sense if you moved in."

"Good," he said. "I'm not clever enough to lead a double life."

Dr. Wall was wearing a new bowtie, a rosebud blossoming big. She imagined him breathing into a mirror while carefully constructing it. Suddenly she said, "I lost my father when I was in grade school and my mother when I was in college. But you know all that, don't you? And we can't forget my Jeffrey." Her eyes, no longer on the doctor's bowtie, rose to his bouncy head of hair. "Most of life is loss. Living with it is hardest."

Dr. Wall spoke. "Especially if you dwell on it."

"My neighbor's cat died, twenty-three years old. I wonder what that calibrates in feline time."

"Old, old, old."

"I'm being a pain in the ass, aren't I? On a positive note, I have a new man in my life. An officer of the law. I'm trying to determine if he's real. If *he* is, I am."

"It sounds serious."

"Could be, unless I'm fooling myself. Tell me that life isn't one big forced smile."

"If I did, Mrs. Comeau, I'm not sure you'd believe me. Or that you should."

They ambled through the park, a fine Sunday, when a scruffy man throwing pieces of bread to pigeons abruptly threw one at her, aiming for her mouth. "He's harmless," Cassidy reassured her. "Has a small mental problem." Farther along they came upon a robustly fat man who regarded her as if she were a meal. "Let's play it safe," she said.

"Let's go home and cuddle."

Bedtime, she asked how Peltinovich was doing with Liam Fitzsimmons, and he said, "She's still enthralled. I told him if he laid an abusive hand on her, I break his face." Deep under the covers their feet touched. "You're a maiden's fantasy, Cassidy."

"*Sir* Cassidy, if you don't mind."

Lights out, the moon high, they were passionate and incautious and not entirely themselves. At the vital moment she shuddered, as if someone had drawn a razor across her throat, the jolt coming from the belief it was lethal. Weeks later a drugstore kit and a physician's confirmation told her she was pregnant. Gazing into a mirror, she scanned a woman nearly out of her thirties but not yet out of her mind. Ultrasound revealed a girl. She and Cassidy wrestled themselves into thick sweaters for a walk. She said, "Marry me."

"I thought you'd never ask."

"And adopt Jeffrey."

That confused him. "A posthumous thing?"

"How else?"

An interlude
THE CHRISTMAS CLARA CRIED

Memory mutes some of the clamor but not Cousin Clara's crying. Nostalgia withers a few facts but not the flavor. Christmas Eve 1941, Roosevelt on the radio, eggnog on the rug at 59 Winter Street, Exeter, New Hampshire.

That was where my great-grandmother lived and where Clara got tipsy and knocked over the Christmas tree in an explosion of burning bulbs, candy canes, and slithering tinsel.

That was where we gathered, a great gust of people, related through blood or marriage, in a house my great-grandfather built with tainted money but didn't live to enjoy—victim of a coronary while still robust and relatively young.

We invaded three downstairs rooms: kitchen, dining room, parlor. Clara floated through all the rooms like a great white wave, her hankie sopping as she greeted late arrivals with mammoth embraces that always lasted a little too long.

My mother's cousin Harold and his wife Eva arrived, a childless couple who belonged to clubs and lodges and traveled throughout the country to conventions. Eva, who wore her blush of pink-blond hair in severe fashion, raised her wrist to reveal a dainty watch Harold had given her, midnight marked by a diamond. Clara shed tears over its beauty.

My paternal grandparents arrived. My grandfather was impolite to Clara. She wept for him, his lack of manners, his thoughtless cruelty, and moments later she wept for me because of my father's dramatic announcement that he was enlisting in the Navy and heading for war. The tears were needless. The Navy, which had accepted him when he was too young, sixteen, and let him serve four peacetime years aboard the *USS Overton*, would not take him now that he was too old, thirty-nine, with a spot on his lung.

My father chatted with Uncle Ralph, who was born to wear a uniform, to hold a stick in his hand and point it at people, to enter rooms without knocking, to make others snap to, and to believe in victory at all costs. He would join the Army, rise in rank, and receive a medal for valor in the Battle of the Bulge. After the war he would join the VFW, fail in the furniture business, and later find morsels of happiness as a hater of hippies and the like. He would lead a charge against a peace march and end up in district court, proud to have blood on his hands again.

Uncle James arrived. Already he'd had one too many and was too jolly, too loud. With him was a quietly attractive woman who for perfectly valid reasons would never marry him. Sensing tragedy, Clara clung to them both and drenched them with overflowing emotions. Uncle James squeezed Clara's hand and then escaped to get a drink. In 1952 he would stroll the forlorn street of some town in Ohio, walking as if rolling on logs, one too many drinks, a comical sight until he fell and hit his head on the curb. A concussion. But the policemen who picked him up wouldn't know this, and in the morning they would find him dead in his cell.

My mother's elder sister arrived with her daughter Dorothy. Dorothy of the impeccable body, seventeen years old, fine honey-colored hair draped to her spine. Clara cried because Dorothy was exquisite. Dorothy drifted among us, aloof, otherworldly, dreaming of modeling dresses and gowns. Instead she would marry an Exeter boy, and my last memory of her would be a hugely pregnant woman with swollen ankles and nothing nice to say about anybody.

My maternal grandmother and her twin sister, deadly rivals since school days, commenced quarreling over whether my great-grandfather, a superintendent at the shoe factory, had forced Polish immigrants to slip him their first week's pay in return for their jobs (which they'd lose six weeks later). One of those immigrants, with many mouths to feed, assaulted my great-grandfather with a wooden shoe last. The incident went unreported, and a month later my great-grandfather died of the coronary.

Soon food was served, buffet, and my mother urged everyone to hurry because there wouldn't be any left, though there was plenty, too much in fact. Clara, nipping brandy, swayed near the Christmas tree, and someone whispered, "Get her away from it."

"I heard that," Clara said, but with a laugh, not a sob. The sob came when she patted my step-brother Richard on the head and told him he had strange and mysterious eyes. Maybe she could see some eleven years into the future when Richard would click his rifle to automatic and empty the magazine into an unarmed Korean, shearing him in half, and come home to brag about it.

Eva was hysterical. She couldn't find the watch Harold had given her. She had slipped it off her wrist to show somebody, and now it was missing. Harold called her an ugly name for her carelessness. People dropped to all fours to look for it. Everybody except James. It was in his hand. He'd had it in his pocket. His joke. Harold wanted to punch him. They raised their fists, James in jest, Harold in dead earnestness. My father lunged between them before one could bruise the other.

In time, the hour late, people began to leave. Fat handshakes were exchanged at the door, along with passionate embraces and some kisses among those who feared they might never see each other again. Long roads to travel. A war in its infancy. The older men could hear distant drums, marching feet, horses' hooves on a wooden bridge. Then we all heard the crash.

Clara and the Christmas tree had joined forces on the floor.

My grandfather wanted to leave her there, but at the same time he feared she'd electrocute herself in the blinking lights or cut herself on the shattered bulbs. My father freed her, and my mother picked tinsel from her hair. Uncle James went outdoors in the cold in search of the woman he had come with, but she had left long ago, a quiet departure only I had noticed.

Within a half-hour the house was empty except for my mother and father, Richard and me, and my great-grandmother and Clara, who had fallen asleep on the couch, a silly-sad smile on her face, as if in sleep she knew that this had been the last gathering at 59 Winter Street.

GINGER

Carl Casper and his wife of twenty-odd years mounted the stairs to an upstairs window to scrutinize their neighbors sunning by a recently installed pool. "At her age," said Betty Casper in reference to their neighbor's wife, "she shouldn't wear her hair so long. How old do you think she is?"

"However old she is," Carl Casper said, "she doesn't look it."

A moment passed. "She cheats on her husband."

"You don't know that for a fact."

"She's the type, you can tell. And we both agree she's a flake. Stuff she writes is off the wall."

"I find it interesting. Sometimes."

Positioned on a chaise, the woman drew her legs up, massaging one calf and then the other as Betty Casper grew conscious of runaway capillaries on her own less shapely legs. Shod in sandals, she noted the need to repaint her toenails and, stepping back, began to cry.

Carl Casper followed her down the stairs. "What the hell's the matter?"

She whirled. "That woman and I are probably the same age, but she looks a damn-sight better than I do. If the two of us were standing side-by-side, men would see her and never notice me."

"You don't know that."

"Don't keep telling me what I don't know." She ran a hand over her jersey. She no longer believed that childbearing marks and a surgical scar gave her abdomen the appearance of a sacred text. "I've had children and paid the price." The Caspers had two sons, both somewhat overgrown. When not at boarding school, they were at summer camp. "*That* woman's never had any."

"You don't know—"

He stopped himself and trailed her into the sort of kitchen seen in magazines.

That woman was born forty-some years ago. Her mother, underage and unmarried, high on a hallucinogen, died during the difficult birth. Her father was anybody's guess. Her grandmother, Millie Karpowicz, called her Ginger, dressed her like a doll, and loved her to pieces.

"There's just the two of us, honey. You and me against the big bad world." Millie Karpowicz was widowed, her husband the victim of an industrial accident, for which she received a sizable settlement, most of it socked away. "We'll never starve, baby. Now look at me and smile."

Ginger Karpowicz was a lovely-looking child and quicker than other girls in her class. In second grade Sister Theresa Marie knelt to her level and said, "You never know your future, Ginger, too many variables. But I'd bet on yours."

"What are variables, Sister?"

"They're like rocks in the road. Learn to go around them."

In the third grade, after a visit to the basement, a euphemism for the toilet, the janitor motioned her to one side and whispered words she knew were bad. "My grandmother says if someone says something like that to me, I should punch hard as I can in the balls."

"That so?" The janitor smiled and loomed over her.

"Then she says I'm s'posed to scream loud as I can."

And she did.

"Who do you think my father was, Nana?"

"I don't think it matters."

"Don't you have any idea?"

"No, and neither did your mother."

"Tell me about my mother."

"Another time, baby. I don't want to be sad."

Wincing when she found Ginger sitting rapt before the TV, lost to a female rock star whose eyes were dime-store gems, Millie Karpowicz dug out old albums. Together they listened to Billie Holiday's *No Regrets* and Peggy Lee's *Where Can I Go Without You.*

"Those are sad, Nana."

"But real, sweetheart. And you can hear the words."

"Did you love Grandpa?"

"All my heart."

At twelve Ginger said to her grandmother, "If I could travel back in time, I'd introduce myself to my mother so we could get to know each other, a little bit anyway."

"You wouldn't get along."

"Why not?"

"She was your age when she lost her dad. He spoiled her silly, and afterward everything I did was wrong, like I didn't even have the right to grieve. The memory of him belonged only to her. Then she started hanging out with the wrong crowd and got into drugs. That's when she stopped knowing me."

"I'm sorry, Nana."

"Traveling back in time is bad business. People would know all the horror ahead and never take a step forward."

Ginger moved from parochial school to public high school and excelled. At a parent-teacher conference Miss Conley, who taught English, greeted Millie Karpowicz warmly and said, "The girl has a superb mind."

Millie Karpowicz beamed. "She got it from her grandfather."

"I wouldn't count yourself out."

Intimidated by Ginger's good looks and brains, most boys kept their distance. Those who approached her failed to impress her—showoffs, mostly jocks who thought they were God's gift, one of whom left lewd notes in her desk. "No originality," she told her best friend, Mary Alice. A top student like herself, Mary Alice would get pregnant by one of the jocks and leave school. Ginger would move on. An associate editor of the school paper, she wrote a teen column that ran Saturdays in the local daily. She was paid by the inch, her grandmother applying a ruler to make sure she wasn't cheated.

The class president, Ambrose Crenshaw III, whose red hair topped his bony height, got up nerve to ask her to the senior prom, and she joined the galaxy of girls in pastel gowns attached to the arms of boys in ill-fitting dinner jackets parading for the cameras in the school gym. After the prom, Ambrose Crenshaw III got fresh, crushing her corsage, as if what he was after was his due, but she promptly put him in his place.

Graduation was held the last week in May under a sky of fair-

weather clouds at the football stadium. Top honors and awards alter-
nated between her and Ambrose Crenshaw III, though Mary Alice,
were she not giving birth, would have taken her share as well.

Millie Karpowicz said, "I'm so proud of you." And, eyes tearing over,
she took a picture of Ginger in cap and gown, diploma in hand.

"What's the matter, Nana?"

"Have I been a good nanny?"

"More than that, you've been a wonderful mum."

"The husband's a cold fish," Betty Casper said.

"That's what bankers are," Carl Casper said. "Their lives revolve
around money. Otherwise they're worthless."

He remembered the day the couple moved in, two loads of fine furniture, their house the nicest in the neighborhood. Expecting to see
children, either teen or pre-teen, he had seen none and merely
glimpsed the husband, who pulled up in a Porsche, conferred briefly
with the movers, and drove off, leaving his wife to oversee. Clad in blue,
she was springtime.

"And she's never been friendly," Betty Casper said.

He was silent.

"Even when I brought over a loaf of banana bread to welcome her
to the neighborhood, she didn't invite me in. Claimed she was working on something. Did you hear me, Carl?"

A lustful adolescent, Carl had imagined nuns out of their habits, not
the nuns who rapped his knuckles in school but those who romped inside his head. Now, hair thinning, waist widening, he lusted after the
woman next door.

"Yes, I heard you," he said, though he hadn't.

"I saw her on her patio the other day. I swear she was smoking a joint.
I mean, you could tell it was a joint by the way she dragged on it."

When the pool went in, he hoped with all his heart that she would
swim *au naturel,* for he had already imagined her as one of his nuns,
but he was disappointed. Her bathing suit was one piece, the kind his
wife wore.

His wife said, "I don't know why the *Valley News* runs that silly col-

umn of hers. And now she's writing under her maiden name. Karpowicz! Her husband probably doesn't want her using his name.
Can't blame him. What do you think she is, Carl? Polish? Jewish?"

"Who cares?"

"I'm just asking, for God's sake."

"No, you're not," and started up the stairs.

"Stuff she writes sounds like she's an atheist."

At his desk, he activated his computer, read an e-mail from a client,
then rose for a pleasure he'd been denying himself. But the woman
wasn't at the pool or anywhere in sight, a deprivation he was con-
templating when he heard his wife.

Her voice struck from behind. "You love her!"

"I *what*?" He sank back to his chair. "I don't even know her."

He spoke to the computer screen, Betty Casper to the back of his head.
"But *I* know you. Last night…."

"What about last night?"

"Were you thinking of her when…."

"What d'you mean?"

"You know exactly what I mean," Betty Casper said and returned to
the stairs.

The computer screen, which had gone blank, returned a confusing
image of someone he didn't know. *Who the hell are you?* It was some man
acquiring an extra chin while losing his hair.

Ginger Karpowicz spent four years at Boston University, during
which time she had two roommates. Both were from New Jersey. One
maintained that the Old Testament god was churlish, the Christian god
a Jew-gilded Greek, Socrates made divine. The other roommate was a
baseball fan who frequently quoted Yogi Berra. *The future ain't what it
used to be.*

Ginger, taking as many literature courses as possible, adored Djuna
Barnes and on a weekend home quoted her favorite line to her grandmother. *Dreams have only the pigmentation of fact.* "What the hell am I
supposed to make of that?" Millie Karpowicz asked.

Ginger quoted an author whose name she couldn't remember. *While we are asleep in this world, we are awake in another; in this way, every man is two men.* "Don't go highfalutin on me, darling. I used to change your shitty diapers."

Her first lover, a teaching assistant with exceptionally clean-cut features, as if computer-enhanced to look all-American, said, "How did you stay a virgin for so long?" The question irked her.

"I was waiting for someone like you." She ran a quick hand down the front of her blouse, checking buttons. "My mistake."

"Don't get mad. How'd you like to marry me?"

"In a pig's ass, as my grandmother would say."

When her next lover, a PhD candidate, didn't work out, she wondered whether sex was special to others but not to her. After the act, she complained, she felt more vanquished than satisfied. One of her roommates said, "You just haven't met the right guy yet. He comes along, you're gonna love it."

In the summer before her final year, she interned at the Boston *Herald* and hated it. It was a tabloid with a predictable attitude, well to the right, and she didn't last. The editor who fired her told her she was in the wrong business.

After graduation she found a basement apartment in Boston's South End and a series of jobs. Editorial assistant at a struggling celebrity magazine that owed her money when it folded. Speechwriter at a high-tech corporation where she dodged the CEO's advances until one evening she agreed to have dinner with him. Afterwards, in his hotel suite, his hands trembled when he touched her, as if she were too great a gift. She came to the same conclusion.

She applied to *Boston World*, a city magazine, and thought she might marry her boss. Though Paul Hannah was already married, that didn't stop her from having dinner with him and listening to the start of a new piece he was working on. *Darwin opened our eyes to the dog-eat-dog world around us, and Freud uncapped our skulls to the horror inside our heads.*

"He's not for you," a coworker told her, and she knew that. When he neglected his meds, his brain misfired fiction for fact and pushed reality down a rabbit hole. "I'm not violent," he said over oysters at Maison Robert. "Just impetuous. Never should've hired you."

"Why not?"

"I was enthralled the moment I laid eyes on you."

"Do you say that to all your female hires?"

"Only beautiful Polacks. And you're the first. Tell me about your hopes and dreams." His face tight in concentration, he gazed at her as if ready to etymologize her every word for the deepest meaning. As if in sickness he had an extra sense.

She said, "It would all be bullshit."

On a visit home, she told her grandmother about him. The good and the bad. "He's brilliant.... He's crazy.... He's...."

Millie Karpowicz was alarmed. "What kind of crazy?"

"Bipolar." Ginger hesitated. "And he's married."

"Good God, girl! What's the matter with you?"

"I love him."

It ended when, with neither warning nor explanation, Paul Hannah disappeared for nine working days. His secretary covered for him, and so did others. On the tenth day he appeared with stitches in his face, nothing he would talk about, though his wife confided to his secretary that police had found him in the street. In the privacy of his office, he said to Ginger, "I'm no good to anyone."

"You don't stay on your meds," Ginger scolded.

"You don't know what it's like. You'd have to be in my head."

"Then help me to understand."

"Help you? How can I help you? I'm fucking buggy."

The day she gave notice, Paul Hannah was sitting at his desk as if in a catatonic daze. She looked in and said, "Are you home?"

He spoke slowly. "Truths, no matter how small, are enormous."

"I'm quitting."

"You prove my point. While breaking my heart."

"May I assume you'll give me a good reference?"

"How can I not? You're my best writer."

Standing on the Cambridge side of the Charles River, against a chill fall wind that sounded like a holler for help and would've bowled her over had she not clutched the rail, she began composing her last piece for *Boston World*. The first line struck a mood.

November is a bone begging for a dog.

The air suggested rain. "My hair," Betty Casper gasped. "I don't want it ruined."

She and an old friend, Phyllis McNulty, hustled through the town parking area to the Lantern Brunch, where they were partial to the omelets. Phyllis McNulty, who had a small inane face and an overlarge bosom, smiled when hers arrived, shot with bits of bacon and onion and loaded with mushrooms. Betty Casper's, ham-and-cheese, was folded inside a huge puff of pastry. Applying a napkin to a corner of her mouth, she said, "I used to be pretty, didn't I? In high school you had the boobs, but I was a beauty."

A little miffed, Phyllis McNulty said nothing.

"I've got some flab on my arms. Don't tell me you haven't noticed."

Phyllis McNulty had. "Not really."

"How's Ed?" Ed was no prize, as Betty Casper knew full well.

Phyllis McNulty dipped into her omelet. "Ed's Ed."

"I don't know who's got it worse—you or me. Carl does most of his work at home now. Hardly ever goes into the office. That's because he likes to peek at our neighbor in her bathing suit. You know who I mean."

"The one who writes for the paper? The banker's wife?"

"If you call that writing. And the banker?" Betty Casper hollowed out her puff of pastry. "He's a cuckold."

Phyllis McNulty glanced up from her omelet.

Betty Casper smiled. "Carl is home today, but she won't be at the pool. It's raining."

Carl Casper was not at home. He was on his neighbor's property. He had seen the husband leave and later, when a light rain began, he watched the wife tool away in her Porsche, the same color as her husband's. Impulsively, he left his house and, breaching a hedge of yews, detected through the mist shrouding the pool the ghost of her presence and the scent of her lotion. Had she materialized, he'd have confessed his love and his lust.

Ornamental trees springing out of tubs lined the patio. The back door was unlocked. Standing inside, he listened carefully, for the house hummed as if she were still in it. Then he forced himself forward. The kitchen was immense, the floor terracotta tile, over which his footsteps echoed. Hung like a weapon was a large frying pan chased with the manufacturer's name, which gave him a start. An intruder, he pictured himself being slammed in the head, his skull reduced to pieces of pottery. *What am I doing here?*

He mounted stairs, the carpeting deadening his steps, his legs trembling. Finding his way to the spacious master bedroom, he breathed in her air, her voice, her doings. He stared hard at the outsize dresser mirror, as if he might retrieve all the images recorded in it, a possibility that thrilled him. Though the bed looked big enough for the whole neighborhood and was too much to behold, he eyed a chest of drawers he was close enough to open and sift through her underthings, but he would never do that. *That's not who I am.*

The bathroom door was ajar. He visualized her in the shower, in the tub, but not on the toilet. Never would he invade her privacy that way. His voice soft, he spoke to her picture on one of the bureaus. "I love you."

She spoke back. *You're quite a guy, Carl.*

Another voice said you're pathetic, that's what you are.

Ginger Karpowicz missed the fifth anniversary reunion of her high school class, the tenth one too, but made it to the fifteenth. Some faces she needed moments to recognize, but there was no mistaking the bony height of Ambrose Crenshaw III, though his red hair had receded. Smoothed back, it looked wet. He told her he was a banker in Boston, lived in a high-rise condo on the waterfront, and was unmarried. "I notice you're not wearing a ring," he said, pleased.

They danced, he somewhat awkwardly. Separating, they mingled, then he joined her at the bar. He bought her a drink and escorted her to a table, where their knees bumped. "Please," he said, "bring me up to date."

She told him about *Boston World* but nothing about Paul Hannah, and spoke about her subsequent two years at the Hartford *Courant* but didn't mention an underheated love affair with a state legislator, which she broke off. She despised being the other woman. She skimmed over stints with the *Morning Call* in Allentown, Pennsylvania, and with the trade magazine in New Jersey. She was back in the area because of her grandmother's deteriorating health.

"She must be pretty old."

"Not that old at all," Ginger said, "but she's had problems."

"Sorry to hear that." He waited a moment, then spoke in a significant voice. "I have to tell you something, Ginger. You did me great honor by letting me take you to the prom. We were Beauty and the Brain. Others began viewing me in a bigger way."

"How odd," Ginger said. "I never thought of you as Beauty."

He smiled, unsure how deep the irony went. "But I should warn you. I'm set in my ways, and I'm not demonstrative."

"Why are you telling me this, Ambrose?"

"I want to be the most important person in your life."

She spoke lightly. "You might have an outside chance of coming in second, but my grandmother's first."

The next day, earlier than usual, she visited her grandmother in the hospital's cardiac care unit. Millie Karpowicz, always trim and well-coiffed, had never looked her age; now she did. Swiftly Ginger leaned over the bed. "How are you doing, Nana?"

"Mind if I don't answer that?" They squeezed hands. Millie Karpowicz's eyes widened. "I look at you, I see your mother if she'd lived."

"I've been so lucky."

"No, I have. I've always had you, but if something happens to me, you'll be alone. I mean, all alone. That's what worries me."

"Then you have to get better."

"No, darling. You'll have to be strong."

A week later Millie Karpowicz died of congestive heart failure. Displayed at the funeral home was the starched face of a dolled-up corpse. Ginger, bent over the casket, wept.

A week after the funeral, Ambrose Crenshaw III proposed marriage, and she accepted. They married in a civil ceremony and left for a honeymoon in Hawaii. Sitting first-class on a jumbo jet and sipping champagne, he said, "Do you love me, Ginger?"

She didn't know but she did take his hand.

In their honeymoon suite they merely fornicated, with little heat, no music. When he said, "Have I disappointed you?" she said, "Don't be silly."

"I'm sure you expected more. You're more experienced."

"You just insulted me, Ambrose."

"I didn't mean to." He was abjectly contrite. "I'll do better next time."

"Don't make a chore of it."

After her move into his Boston condo, they tried to have a child, an Ambrose IV if a son, but she failed to conceive. He was uncomfortable discussing the matter, and neither sought medical advice. She moved on to other things, teaching a journalism course at Bunker Hill Community College and freelancing for *Boston World*, long under new editorship. Where was Paul Hannah? No one seemed to know or care, but the new editor liked her first submission in which she called the new office buildings rising along the harbor elaborate show fortresses, more military than corporate in their pomp.

Dining in a North End restaurant, about which she was writing a piece, her husband leaned over his pasta and asked if she had ever smoked marijuana. "A few times," she said. "When I was young."

"I never have."

She tore bread and buttered a chunk. "Why are you asking me this, Ambrose?"

"Promise you'll never make a fool of me."

"Why would I do that?"

He didn't know. "Forgive me," he said.

A year later, in the same restaurant, he told her he was sick of Boston, fed up with unnerving traffic, clogged tunnels, the choked bridges. Ginger said, "Tell me what you want to do."

He'd had offers, and after a lengthy negotiation he was named investment officer at Bradford Trust in Haverhill, a move that took them both back to their roots, though he preferred that they live in nearby Andover, a tony town suitable for a man of his standing. He chose the house, the most impressive in the neighborhood, with all the luxuries and extras, except for a swimming pool. "I can remedy that," he told her.

He thought it advantageous if she joined things in town. Friends of the Library, for instance. She saw no problem with that. He listed other things. "Don't overload me, Ambrose. I'm a working woman." She didn't have to be, he reminded her. "Trust me, Ambrose. I do." Reluctantly she agreed to accompany him to services at the Congregational church on Elm Street, where the minister expounded on perfect bliss awaiting the faithful. On the way out, Ginger shook the minister's hand. "I loved your sermon, Reverend, but keep in mind that malcontents are everywhere. If there's a heaven, we're sure to find some there."

Walking toward his Porsche, her husband said, "That wasn't necessary."

"For me it was."

Sitting by the pool, she took a call on her cell phone and felt her shoulders tense. The voice, which she recognized at once, was Paul Hannah's. A moment later, she stopped him. "I'm married, Paul."

"I know. I've Googled you through the years. You've moved around but I've kept up."

"Apparently. And you, where are you now?"

"*Valley News.*" He paused. "I know, it's a comedown."

She felt bad for him. It was a struggling local weekly, a throwaway, with real estate ads.

"I could use your help, Ginger. Hear me out before you say anything. Write a column for me, something offbeat, controversial, any topic you want. I need to spice the paper up, get people reading it." When she didn't answer, he said, "Don't make me beg."

She got her best ideas by the pool, the sun in her face, eyes closed. In her second column, the minister in mind, she equated Christian hubris with male chauvinism in giving God a human face and making it masculine. Heaven she defined as the sum of all good memories tainted by none of the terrible ones, and ended with her own kind of irony. *If we stood face to face with God, we would become fiction and God would become fact.*

Paul Hannah thought it even better than her first. Her husband said, "Please don't embarrass me."

"I'll use my maiden name."

"Good."

She had a drink with Paul Hannah in the lounge at the Andover Inn. She ate her olive and then his. After they clinked glasses, he said, "I've never gotten over you."

"Time you did. Are you on your meds?"

"You are my meds."

Carl Casper stood at the upstairs window. Leaves were turning, birds departing in a sky of traveling clouds. His wife, coming up the stairs, said, "She won't be at the pool much longer."

He headed for his office. "She's not there now. Probably won't be again. Pool's covered over."

Betty Casper spoke from the top of the stairs. "Poor baby. Can't fill your eyes anymore with Polish pastry."

Ensconced at her computer, Ginger Karpowicz wrote of lost leaves and changing seasons. *Autumn is the autopsy of summer.* Ambrose Crenshaw III said, "Why can't you write things that matter to people?"

One evening Carl Casper followed Ginger Karpowicz from a distance while never totally losing sight of her Porsche until she ran a red light. He made quick turns and, God guiding him, glimpsed the Porsche settled in near the Andover Inn. Parked well away, he watched every step of her stride along a pathway and waited several minutes before following. Inside the lounge, he spotted her sitting with a man who looked neither reliable nor reasonable.

You could do better. You could have me!

On a bright November day Paul Hannah said, "So this is where you live." Her computer was on the fritz, and he had stopped by to pick up her column. "Beautiful place." Trailing her into the room she used as an office, he glanced out the window at the covered-up pool. "Nifty. Just walk out the back and dive in. Ever swim in the buff?"

She shook her head. "I suspect my neighbors are voyeurs." Before she could react, he stepped toward her, and in the next moment she was solid in his arms. She said, "Where are we going with this, Paul?"

"Are we talking minutes or years?"

"One is apples and the other oranges."

Over omelets at the Lantern Brunch, Betty Casper said, "He's cheating on me in his head."

"Better there than in the Polack's bed," Phyllis McNulty said.

"She wouldn't give him a second look. You'd think he'd know that." Betty Casper watched a man dip a doughnut into his coffee and eat the wet part. "It's getting out of hand. I think he's stalking her."

"Jesus, Betty. He could get himself in trouble."

"This is what I have to put up with. And there could be something worse, but I won't go into it."

Phyllis McNulty reached out and patted her friend's ring-encrusted hand. "You have to do something."

"I know that."

"A word to the wise might work," Phyllis McNulty advised.

Ambrose Crenshaw III was perusing the annual report of an up-and-coming company in the Midwest when his secretary stepped into his office and spoke in lowered tones. A woman was on the line, wanted to speak to him but wouldn't say who she was. Said it was important. An emergency. He took the call, and a woman said, "Things are going on with your wife that you should know about. I'll say no more."

And Betty Casper didn't.

Her computer repaired, Ginger Karpowicz was forwarding a couple of columns in advance to Paul Hannah. She wanted a lull, time to think, time not to think. In the first column she posed a question. *Are we closer to the monkey than the monkey is to us?* She knew that Paul Hannah would like the piece, but perhaps no one else would. The second piece was written with her grandmother in mind. *Death, though a dear friend at the end, is the stranger we live with all our lives.*

She and her husband attended Sunday service, at the conclusion of which the minister stationed himself at the door and said, "What words of wisdom do you have for me today, Mrs. Crenshaw?"

Ginger smiled. "Let's face it, Reverend, the whole of Heaven may not be worth a single day on Earth."

On the way to their car, his Porsche, her husband said, "Still up to your tricks, I see." At home his voice turned darker and deeper on a different subject. "This editor of yours, this Hannah, you worked for him before?"

"Long time ago."

"I checked up on him. He's a loony."

She closed the door of the closet where she had hung her coat. He still had his on. "And why did you check up on him, Ambrose?"

"Is there a reason I shouldn't have?"

"Shows a lack of trust."

He removed his topcoat. Slung over his shoulders, empty arms dangled as if they had a life of their own. "Has Hannah ever been in this house?"

"I told you when. The time I had the problem with the computer."

An odd smile made his mouth look broken. "Did you have sex with him?"

That's what a man and a woman do. "Of course not."

A chilly Monday, snow already in the air. Watching her drive off to her weekly hair appointment, Carl Casper waited five minutes and entered through the patio, heading straight up the staircase to the master bedroom to breathe her air, her smells. He was not the sort to paw lingerie, but what was the harm? His fingers caressed underpants not unlike his wife's. Impulsively he shed his shirt, his shoes, and then, at full throttle, everything else. Seized with a smile, he stumbled to the mirror that stored her images and added his own.

The huge bed waited, no one to stop him. Throwing back the spread, casting aside top covers, he found her side. No mistaking that. His senses told him so and his skin verified it. Conjuring up her warmth, he embraced her as only a lover could. Phantom thighs clenched him, calves locked him in, the sounds of pleasure half hers.

The owner of the hair salon, a woman named Barbara, was reshaping Ginger Karpowicz's hair this week, coloring to come. Catching Ginger's eye in the mirror, she said, "You know I always read your column, Mrs. Crenshaw, but I don't always know what you're saying."

"I don't always know myself."

Barbara stepped back a moment to view her progress. "Do you believe all those things you write?"

"When I'm writing them, I do. Later I may wonder."

She ran a smoothing hand over Ginger's hair. "You said shadows are blackboards that can't bear the weight of chalk. I'm just curious. What does that mean?"

"Doesn't have to mean anything, Barbara. Just has to sound nice."

"You look sad, Mrs. Crenshaw."

"Do I? Actually I'm happy."

Guiding his Porsche into his driveway, Ambrose Crenshaw III pulled to a stop and proceeded through the chilly dusk, topcoat over his shoulders, sleeves flapping. Entering his house, the sounds brought him to a long halt. His overcoat puddling to the entry hall carpet, all his senses put to work, he moved to the closet door, opened it, then turned, climbing the staircase, fully loaded revolver in hand.

In the master bedroom, hairy legs hung from sheets, as did a hairy ass.

"Where is she?"

It took a moment to recognize the face that presented itself, mouth agape, as the one that belonged, not to Paul Hannah, but to his fat-assed neighbor. And a moment longer for the nature of her days with this idiot, this piece of shit, to clarify into the knowledge of her skill at making a fool of him. He aimed the revolver chest high.

"It's not what you think it is," Carl Casper gasped.

"It never is." He tightened his hold on the revolver. Might even have cocked it as Carl Casper began to cry.

"Where is she!" He stepped across the threshold. "In her bathroom?"

"It's Monday," Carl Casper sobbed. "She's not here. Please don't hurt me."

"Shut up!"

The blob was taking up more than his fair share of space, breathing more air than he was entitled to. "Get out."

Frantically, gratefully, Carl Casper started to dress.

"No!" He waved the revolver. "Take your clothes with you!" Carl Casper stumbled out of the bedroom. Slipped and skidded. Almost tumbled down the stairs. Left by the patio. Dropped a shoe and a sock in the kitchen. Didn't matter. Nothing mattered.

Ambrose Crenshaw III cautiously descended the staircase, seated himself on the bottom stair, and, holding the revolver with the hammer at the ready, waited for his wife to come home.

GEORGE W. BUSH

On a windy day in April, the sun brightening the bark of old trees, Ellen Burnside and her husband Teddy drove to town hall, where lawyers awaited them. They were selling Teddy's mother's house, which had fallen into disrepair during her final years. Teddy, still grieving, anticipated the sale with no enthusiasm while Ellen, looking to the future, viewed it with much. After months of dickering with brokers and potential buyers, she had gotten a good offer, though the net would be modest. The house was mortgaged. Before stepping out of the car, Ellen inspected her face in a compact mirror and gave a touch to her dark hair. Forebears on her father's side included a French-Canadian fur trader and an Indian maiden who had mingled their defiant blood and, working through the generations, gave Ellen her beauty, which always dazzled Teddy, to the point of worship. Snapping shut her compact, she said, "I'm ready."

"I'm not," Teddy confessed.

"Take a deep breath."

Their lawyer met them inside the century-old brick building and ushered them into a high-windowed room, where they seated themselves at a library table that smelled of varnish. The buyers were not present, just as well. Teddy did not want to come face to face with strangers taking over his childhood home. The buyers' lawyer, sitting across from them, had a meager moustache, like fine print. Openly admiring Ellen's features, he said, "I congratulate you, Mrs. Burnside. You're a hard bargainer." He readjusted his horn-rims and added, "Especially for someone so young."

Not all that young. She was approaching thirty, her face an oval of seeming indifference. She watched their lawyer lay out documents for Teddy to sign, her signature unneeded. Teddy's fingers froze on the pen. His mother had given him fair hair and baffling blue eyes that at the moment expressed nothing.

"Teddy." Ellen's whisper was gossamer sheathing steel. "Either sign it or put the pen down." ("Shit or get off the pot" is what her father would have said.)

In the room's silence Teddy smiled through a tide of noise in his head
not unlike the one concocted when his boyhood set of lead soldiers had
fought enemies to the finish to preserve perimeters. He worked the pen
lightly and produced the line of an ocean wave as in a child's drawing.
Swiftly a certified check was provided.

"Take it, Teddy."

"You take it," he said with the eyes of an orphan, his voice distant,
not altogether his own.

The buyers' lawyer, whose attention had never wavered, watched
Ellen fold the check and slip it into her bag. "I don't know where you
got your smarts, Mrs. Burnside, but you ought to get into real estate.
You'd do well, guaranteed."

Everybody rose at once, except Teddy, who had sunk deep in his chair
and needed time. Ellen handed him his jacket. When his left arm
snagged in the sleeve, she helped him make it right. A thread trailed
from the worn cuff. "Thank you," he murmured.

Outside, the wind challenged them. Ellen's hair blew back and
Teddy's came apart as they hustled to their car, a Dodge in need of work.
"I'll drive," Ellen said, not always patient with his driving, which was
cautious and tentative, though once it had been reckless. Inside the car,
she reexamined the check, drawn on Kenwood Trust Company. "Money
makes money."

Teddy looked at her profile. "Is that what it's all about?"

"I want things to be good for us."

"I'm vulnerable," he said.

"Everybody's vulnerable."

"Shouldn't be that way."

"Should or shouldn't doesn't enter into it."

Trailing smoke, she drove up Front Street, past the Kenwood Inn,
seven years ago the scene of their wedding reception, a happy time; past
fine old houses that reluctantly gave way to lesser ones; and beyond
to Kenwood High School, where Teddy no longer enjoyed teaching. Cell
phones that should've been turned off disrupted his classes, girls with
bare midriffs and trinkets in their navels distracted him, and colleagues kept their distance because they didn't always know what to
make of him.

"Let me have the check," he said when she pulled up near the school's side entrance.

She gave him a curious look and no argument. A few days ago he had suggested a scholarship in his mother's name, not a pleasing idea, which her face had instantly shown. Abruptly he flipped the check over, endorsed it, and returned it. "Will this make things better?"

"It can't hurt."

He climbed out of the Dodge into the mean-spirited wind, his hair pulling from its part. Holding the door open, he looked back in and forgot what he had intended to say, as if from elisions in his memory. He wanted more elisions. Full forgetfulness.

"What's the matter?" Ellen asked.

"I don't know who I am."

"Of course you do. You're Teddy."

Her appointment was at two-thirty. Without apology, he kept her waiting a half hour. His name was Jack O'Grady, and he was executive vice president of the venerable Kenwood Trust Company, though he contrasted sharply with the subdued décor. Portly in a fawn suit, he had a bluff ungovernably Irish face, a split chin, and a hard head of grizzled hair. She imagined him tugging a comb through it. His accent was South Boston, and his employment in Kenwood was an admission by the directors that the bank needed new blood, bigger ideas, and a more aggressive posture.

"Have a seat, Mrs. Burnside."

The chair stationed her squarely before his impressive desk, as if she were being granted an audience with someone much weightier than a mere money man. His eyes appraised her in a way that appealed to her vanity, which she promptly dismissed. An eighth-grade teacher had once likened vanity to a mirror, the reflection always favorable and invariably false. The teacher told her that the day she wore a tight sweater to school.

"Thank you for seeing me," she said.

He had her husband's check on his desk. Turning it over, he looked at the ocean line that passed for a signature. Then he flipped it back to the business side and reread an amount insignificant to him, not to her. In her childhood there had rarely been a time when money wasn't an urgency.

"So," he said, fluttering the check, "you want to play with this."

Ellen held her chin high. "I don't play with money, Mr. O'Grady."

"But *I* do." His eyes flew at her over a smile that was pure Irish but only half blarney. "For me, money is a game, not a matter of life or death. If I go belly-up, I only play dead. Nobody's looking, I'm back on my feet. Story of my life. I tell you this so you'll know who you're talking to. How old are you, Mrs. Burnside?"

She ignored the question, along with the self-aggrandizement, and glanced at her watch, a clear message that her age was irrelevant, her time was not. Challenged, he saturated her with a long look.

"Shouldn't your husband be here?"

"No," she said simply.

"Why me, Mrs. Burnside? Why'd you specifically ask to see me?"

"I've heard interesting things about you."

"Good or bad?"

"Both."

O'Grady's smile stood out at full strength. "Let me explain what I am, Mrs. Burnside, then draw your own conclusions. I'm an investment banker. I deal. I package. You've heard about the goose that lays the golden egg. I poke a finger into the goose and if I feel an egg coming I invest. That means a triple partnership—me, the bank, and the client. Still want to talk to me, Mrs. Burnside?"

For a nanosecond she did not. "Is what you're saying legal?"

"You tell me."

He was baiting her, bullying her, amusing himself at her expense, which she felt was a small price if it meant a stake in the future. At the same time, less appealing, he reminded her of an uncle who had inappropriately displayed affection. *Bad man*, she later told her dolly.

Now it was O'Grady consulting his watch, an unsubtle reminder that time, especially his, was money. "All right, let's hear what you've got in mind," he said, and in a tone of unbridled confidence she described a stretch of property on Portsmouth Avenue, quiet farmland leading out of town toward the New Hampshire coast, in her estimation prime for development. His smile made her suspect she was telling him nothing he didn't know. He said, "If I read you right, you want to play with the big boys."

"Anything wrong with that?"

All business, he rose from his desk. On his feet he was not as tall as she'd expected, and she waited for him to add something to himself. The fawn suit made him more a bookie than a banker. "You got balls, Mrs. Burnside."

The reference didn't offend her. "What I have, Mr. O'Grady, is a brain."

"Let's go see the property."

His car was a Lexus, top of the line. Anything less would have surprised her, though she was unprepared for the large fur dice dangling inside. A nick in the windshield reminded her that nothing in life is perfect. She buckled up, O'Grady didn't. Downtown, he maneuvered around the bandstand and, tapping the horn, cut into traffic as if the street were his. Haley's TV & Appliances announced a sale, and the Ioka was showing a Nicole Kidman movie. Ellen, who'd taken accounting courses at the community college, did the books for both businesses.

"Bet you'd like to own this town, wouldn't you, Mrs. Burnside?"

"A piece. I'm not greedy."

"Greed is good. Some movie said so."

The sky swooped down on them when they stepped from the Lexus to scan an expanse of tilled soil. Within sight was a farmhouse near which forsythia gushed into bloom and beyond that a barn with birds spurting off the roof. Ellen pointed. "The property extends past that rise."

"I know where it goes."

She had sudden second thoughts. It was Teddy's money she'd be risking. "I suppose there's no rush."

"If the time's right, Mrs. Burnside, you don't wait. You act. You go into hock if you have to. That's not something I really need to tell you, is it?" He was staring at her from the tail of his eye, viewing her in a way that had nothing to do with the matter at hand. "You got kids?" he asked suddenly.

"No."

"I got two sons. One's putting his life on the line in Iraq. The other's studying quantum mechanics at MIT. Do you know what a neutrino is?"

"Do I need to?"

"It sounds like some kind of fruit. That's how much I know."

The wind shifted, and the smell of the tilled field turned powerful, like skunk. They returned to the Lexus and sat quietly as the electric windows sealed themselves with the smallest sound. Settled into the leather upholstery, O'Grady was at home. "There was a time, Mrs. Burnside, I had money only for the vitals, nothing for the fancies. Now I crave the fancies." He was staring at her, again from the far edge of his eye. "You're a beautiful woman, you know that? A genuine doll."

"That's not who I am, Mr. O'Grady. The same as you're not just a big thatch of hair and a dangling pair of dice. What about the property?"

"That check of yours is next to nothing."

"We've been through that."

"I know what the farmer's asking. It's too much."

"Who's going to beat him down?"

O'Grady switched on the ignition, and the engine spoke before he did. "You are."

The Lexus carried them a short distance up the highway to the un-paved drive of the farmhouse, a two-story clapboard structure with a screened-in porch. A dog of no particular breed picked itself up from the front steps to bark as the Lexus purred to a stop. The forsythia glared. Before opening her door, Ellen said, "Are you going to be both my banker *and* my partner?"

"Before I answer that, let's see how you do."

At first, not well. The farmer was foxier than he looked, but gradually, ensconced in a parlor decorated with samplers, O'Grady silently looking on, Ellen brought the farmer down to a price that pleased her and didn't entirely displease him. O'Grady's demeanor divulged nothing.

At the breakfast table Teddy Burnside said, "Do we know what we're doing?"

"Trust me."

He always had, he always would. "I just thought it might be fun to open a book store."

"The chains would choke us. We'd be broke in a year."

Teddy added peanut butter to his toast. "What sort of man is O'Grady?"

"The sort who can make things happen."

For a transparent moment, without knowing why, Teddy felt threatened. "He sounds interesting."

Always attuned to nuances, Ellen spoke quickly. "How interesting can he be? He's a money man." She trained her eyes on her husband to better study the situation. "How are you feeling, Teddy. Your head on straight? What time is your appointment?"

Automatically Teddy looked at his watch. "Not till ten."

At ten, Teddy was locked in a leather chair that threatened to swallow him while Dr. Wall reigned from behind a mahogany desk. Each was taking note of the other, and each was a careful listener, as if everything said was in a code that needed to be cracked. Dr. Wall, his eyes embedded in his horn-rims, said, "How are you feeling today, Mr. Burnside? Your head on straight?"

"My wife asked me that." Teddy was on the alert. Perhaps the doctor knew something he didn't. He thought the unthinkable and was unable to unthink it. "My wife's seeing another man."

"Are you sure?"

"Not absolutely," he conceded with a smile and wondered how the errant thought had entered his head in the first place. He stared at the doctor's bowtie, a flourish of polka dots, obviously hand-tied, not clipped on. The doctor was real. He was not. He was sealed inside an inner world and groping with scenes that dissolved before fully developed. "I'm sick," he said.

"We must do something about that."

He was coping with an image too garish to bleach from his mind. A bird pecked the cupped hand of a little girl lying roadside with an open skull and a broken cage of ribs. Her mother lay here and there.

"Staying on your meds, Mr. Burnside?"

Held too long, his smile began to hurt, and at once he imagined birds bursting into flight, himself one of them. Sky's the limit. His head heard a gull's cry or a woman's scream, nothing to distinguish one from the other. The doctor's bowtie quivered.

Dr. Wall spoke sharply. "Do me a favor, Mr. Burnside. Stop smiling."

"I can't."

Jack O'Grady was in love with her, which happened fast, but not so fast she didn't see it coming. Over lunch at the Kenwood Inn, ostensibly to talk business, O'Grady tried to possess her with his eyes, but she'd have none of it. "At least tell me something about yourself," he said.

What was there to tell? No need to bring up an uncle drawn to girls, twelve the perfect age. Then there was her father, reactionary, bellicose, unable to hold a job. Should she mention that, like her father, her husband bought used cars that backfired into extinction? A positive comparison lay between her and her grandmother and the pride they shared in their distant Indian blood. Way back when, Nana didn't vote for Kennedy because, she said, a man with his finger on the nuclear button should be an atheist, someone who knows there's no happy hunting ground.

"So did you vote for Nixon, Nana?"

"That son-of-a-bitch? I voted for no one."

O'Grady said, "Why are you smiling?"

She didn't know she was. "I thought we came here to talk business."

"It's a done deal. Don't worry about it."

She poked a fork into her garden salad while he jabbed at his. "Is what we're doing legal?" she asked quietly.

"Everything concerning you is on the up-and-up. Anything silly falls on me. Feel better?" A cell phone chimed inside his suit. He carried two. "It's my kid. The one in Iraq." He excused himself and left the table to talk in private. Proud of both sons, he clearly was closest to the one in uniform. Ten minutes later he returned with a tear in his eye and feral pride in his voice. "It's a war we have to win. No fucking choice. Excuse the language."

Ellen said nothing. Her nana, way back when, told her that war tainted everybody, molested women and children and, leaving no lasting winners, shrank all victories. Nana told of the nightly news leading off with body bags and kill counts. Different war. Different time. Everything else the same.

"I feel so much for this kid of mine," Grady said and resumed jabbing a salad that no longer looked appetizing. A cord stuck out on his neck when he pointed his fork at her. The tines looked lethal. "Doesn't mean I'm not proud of my other boy, a smart little bastard, but what do I know about quarks and neutrinos? I mean, who does?"

Teddy had caused himself trouble with the school committee for defining war as the blind dropping bombs and the deaf yelling at each other. He had chalked on the blackboard what he told his class were the two most evil words in the English language. *Halliburton* and *ExxonMobil.* He wasn't fired, but he was warned.

Their lunch arrived, but O'Grady no longer wanted his. He put his fork down and ordered a second martini. "Don't mind, do you?" he said and took pleasure in his martini, though his face didn't show it. The red bullet in his mouth was his tongue. "Please don't tell me you're a Bush basher, Mrs. Burnside. Tell me you're not one of those leftwing fanatics."

In a quiet moment Teddy had told her that war was no longer Bang Bang. It was Boom Boom. Wholesale. Indiscriminate. Bulging with road kill. The world a septic tank sucking up horrors. She lifted her water glass. "My husband was in Iraq."

O'Grady acted as if blindsided, betrayed. "Why didn't you say so?"

"I didn't want to get into a discussion."

Teddy's gaze locked onto the prettiest girl in the classroom, Jennifer, who sat slouched in low-slung jeans that exposed the sparkle in her navel, her glossy hair as long as Ellen once wore hers, but Ellen had allowed nothing in her navel except his tongue, his passion almost shameful. Tearing his eyes from Jennifer's midriff, he opened his tattered copy of *The Red Badge of Courage.* All had been assigned to read it, but he suspected few had. "If Crane teaches us anything," he said in his classroom voice, "it's that the fittest don't necessarily survive." A cell phone rang. So did Teddy's head. "Please turn that off."

A boy deep in the back did, arm raised, hand dangling like bait. "You were in Iraq, isn't that so, sir? Were you a hero?"

Teddy's head continued to ring. As if something nearby had detonated. Memory of a fellow Guardsman who, sick of it all, activated a grenade, kept it in his hand, and smiled. *Get rid of it! Get rid of it!* Instead the grenade got rid of him.

Jennifer raised her hand, from the elbow. Sweet luscious Jennifer. The fire on her mouth was lipstick. Ellen at sixteen. "You OK, Mr. Burnside?"

He spoke to her navel. "The dead wait for us to die so they won't be bothered by our memories of them."

Did that make sense? Apparently not, for the boy deep in the back, hand fluttering again, shouted, "What's that got to do with anything, sir?"

Teddy strode to the blackboard and chalked, *Bang. Bang. Boom. Boom.* Then: *Bush. Bush.*

Jack O'Grady drove her to a harbor restaurant in Portsmouth, where they met with a developer of shopping malls, whose questions Ellen answered confidently and succinctly. O'Grady, consuming lobster without a bib, was increasingly struck by her poise and presence. Worried he might get caught gazing at her like a dog with its tongue out, he studied a stain on his silk necktie.

"Try club soda," the developer advised, interrupting himself. Like O'Grady, he wore a lapel pin of stars and stripes.

"Better yet," Ellen said, "throw it away."

At evening's end, O'Grady laid out a credit card, one of many wedged into a wallet branded with his monogram. The developer, whose small expressionless eyes were monosyllables, spoke almost without moving his mouth to O'Grady rather than to Ellen. "I'll give you an answer after my accountant runs over the figures."

Ellen stared at the developer's face and disliked every bit of it. "We'd like the answer as soon as possible."

On the drive back to Kenwood, the moon a light-second away, she stared at the Lexus's dashboard as if it were the universe in miniature, messages beaming in from afar. "You've done business with that guy before," she said.

O'Grady shrugged. "Once or twice."

"A lot I don't know, isn't there?"

"And a lot *I* don't know. What was your husband doing in Iraq? He's no kid, is he?"

"He was when he joined the Guard. It gave him money for college. The money got better as he rose in rank, so he stayed in. And that's how he got grabbed for Bush's war."

"So it wasn't for God and country, only for the money."

"It's always for the money. You're a banker, you should know that."

Color cruised into O'Grady's face. "Why are you so cynical, Mrs. Burnside? No, don't answer that. None of my business. Just let me say, we got guys getting blown to bits in Baghdad and it ain't for the fucking money." He slanted the Lexus around the bandstand, proceeded up High Street, and slowed as they approached the Kenwood Inn. "Look, we shouldn't argue. We're partners. You game for a nightcap?" She wasn't. Not surprised but keenly disappointed, he drove on with eyes not on the road but fastened on her. "It's obvious how I feel about you. Goddam gorgeous is what you are." The Lexus neared a turn. "Don't worry, I have peripheral vision. Someone said you got Indian blood. True?"

"Not pertinent, Mr. O'Grady."

"Everything about you is pertinent. You were mine, I'd give you the world."

"Not yours to give."

He made another turn, which led to a cul-de-sac of bungalows, hers the second on the left, streetlight revealing meager grass on its poorly sodded front lawn. No lights in the windows, no sign of anybody. "Where's your husband?" he asked, and she murmured, "School committee." Without ever having met him, O'Grady considered Teddy Burnside generic, could be anybody's husband, his sole cachet marriage to a beauty with squaw blood. "Can I come in for a minute? See if I can get the stain out of my necktie."

"Your wife can do that."

"We don't see eye to eye."

"Thank you for dinner, Mr. O'Grady."

And she was gone, vanishing into the dark of the bungalow, into the maw of her private life. A light went on, a shade was pulled, her silhouette visible one moment and not the next. O'Grady drew pictures of her in his mind. His doll. His papoose. When he stepped from the Lexus, a stiff breeze slapped his face. The bungalow's front step was loose, and the screen door had a tattered hole. He tried the inside door, which opened with ease, and called her name. He heard something but wasn't sure what. He trailed his fingers over the arm of a plush chair worn at the edges and let carpeting soften his footsteps as he followed his instincts toward a small light in an open room. Stopping short, he held his breath and savored the sight of flared hips, tapered thighs, and private hair running rampant.

"Hello," he said.

She screamed.

The school committee talked to Teddy in closed session. The chairman, Dr. Tagget, said, "We are all aware that you served honorably in Iraq."

"I served neither honorably nor dishonorably," Teddy said in a voice meant for a classroom, not a small conference room. "I served, period."

"Of course."

"Of course what?"

With a swift glance, Dr. Tagget sought help from one of his colleagues, Mrs. Langevin, a widow in wonderful repair, her perfume imbuing the room. Teddy scrutinized the two of them. The hair on Dr. Tagget's prominent head was slight, hardly worth the bother, while Mrs. Langevin's hair, rigid with spray, was a bouquet. Teddy wondered whether the two had ever been intimate and ruled against it.

Mrs. Langevin said, "Would you like a sabbatical, Mr. Burnside? I'm sure it could be arranged."

"Why don't we get to the crux of the matter?" Teddy said. "Why am I here?"

Dr. Tagget took charge again. "Simply put, you don't have a right to foist your political views on your class. You've been told this before. Your job is to teach American literature, not partisan politics."

"Is that what I'm doing?" Teddy asked, but his words didn't carry. He pressed the back of his fist against his mouth, hurting his teeth the way he had when crouching over the driver of a Humvee hit by rocket fire. The driver lay in the sand, a portion of him already vegetable, imminent death a mere formality.

Mrs. Langevin said, "Not to flatter you, Mr. Burnside, but you're a handsome man. Females in your class must be distracting, especially the way they dress."

"One in particular, your niece Jennifer, has an exquisite navel. Like my wife's."

Mrs. Langevin turned on him with a look of disgust and contempt. Dr. Tagget said, "We'll arrange your sabbatical. Perhaps a permanent one."

"I have tenure."

After a knowing glance at Mrs. Langevin, Dr. Tagget said, "No, Mr. Burnside. Technically you don't."

Jack O'Grady was in the kitchen washing blood from his face. Goddamit, he had meant no harm, but without warning she had struck with her nails, a warrior of a woman. Wearing a robe cinched at the waist and pulled tight at the throat, she stood near the fridge with folded arms. Neither noticed Teddy in the doorway until he spoke.

"What happened? Who's this man?"

Ellen said without inflection, "The banker. He made a mistake— didn't you, Mr. O'Grady? Mr. O'Grady has a son in Iraq."

Teddy wasn't buying anything. He stared at Ellen. "Did he assault you?"

"You kidding me?" O'Grady said, ripping loose sheets of paper toweling. "She assaulted *me!* Look at my fucking face."

Teddy despised vulgar language in front of his wife. Had he an automatic weapon in his hands and had he not sworn against killing of any kind, he'd have blasted O'Grady to kingdom come. In a heartbeat. As he and others in a panic or a rage had done to a family of four. Impossible to tell which. Who knew? Who knew anything?

Ellen gave O'Grady a loose look. "We still have a deal?"

"Money's money."

Teddy said, "I can't let this pass."

"Of course you can," Ellen said and made a shooing motion to O'Grady, who ripped off more paper toweling and left without further word. Teddy took a seat at the dinette table and watched Ellen load up Mr. Coffee and trigger it for the morning. She said, "We don't need to talk about this now, do we?"

"No." He brought his hands together and rested them on the table. "They don't want me to teach anymore."

"Big surprise."

The nerve fibers of his brain were doing him a disservice, letting numerous selves war inside him and mess with him in a manner that had led to his release from active duty and his discharge from the Guard. Home free.

"What is it, Teddy? Whatever it is, say it."

"We never should've sold my mother's house. That house was who I was."

Ellen believed in tough love. "Now you're someone else. Let's live with it."

A few months passed before Teddy went back to see Dr. Wall, who was wearing a familiar bowtie. Teddy remembered the polka dots. Ensconced in the large leather chair and glancing at family pictures on Dr. Wall's desk, Teddy felt comfortably at home. "I have questions for you, Doctor. I've been saving them up. Can truth stand the test of time?"

"That's yet to be decided."

"But what do you think?"

"Truth, like God, is human architecture. But that's merely an opinion."

"People tend to die with their eyes open. Are they trying to grab a last look?"

"I wouldn't be surprised." Dr. Wall's round face refused to be read and when viewed too long tended to turn simple.

Teddy said, "Bush is a boy playing with toy soldiers that bleed."

"That's not a question."

Teddy resorted to an old habit of vanishing inside himself, where no one, not even his conscious self, could follow. He never stayed there long. Too dark. Too dangerous. He gripped the plump arms on the leather chair and yanked himself forward in an effort to sit straight. "My wife has a bit of Native American blood. It gives her authenticity others lack. You and I, Doctor, aren't absolutely real, but she is. I like your tie."

"Thank you. Are you staying on your meds?"

"More or less. I'm no longer a teacher, Doctor. My wife and I have become entrepreneurs. It's the American way."

A bubble burst in Jack O'Grady's brain. Happened during business hours at the bank. Elbows on his desk, he placed both hands on his forehead and slumped forward without so much as a goodbye. "Dead as a doornail," the emergency medical technician murmured to his assistant.

The elder son came home from Iraq in full-dress uniform to attend his father's funeral. His brother picked him up at the airport in the Lexus and drove him to the family home, a flag pitched over the front door. Each brother raised a hand and snapped off a salute, an O'Grady tradition. The younger brother had tears in his eyes. The older one had none. He had seen too much. "We all go," he said quietly. "Some sooner."

"I loved him."

"I didn't," the older brother said and snapped off a second salute that may have mocked the first. Hard to tell.

JOCELYN

Who came up with the idea to run naked through the pine grove behind Kenwood Academy? Who but Jocelyn? She had the balls, the boys didn't. She was eleven, the boys a full year older. Raymond had a flop of hair across his forehead while Winston, albino without clothes, had a wiffle. Flaxen locks flying, Jocelyn led the frolic through spokes of sunlight over a carpet of needles. Raymond was hard on her heels, followed by Winston. Galloping, losing ground, Winston skidded, slipped, and tumbled ass over teakettle. He rose cautiously, indignantly, and went behind a blueberry bush to pee.

The sound of a hornet beating its wings hovered near Jocelyn's ear as she confronted fern fronds and slashed through them like a warrior princess, two knights in her service, one momentarily indisposed. Birch trunks simulated the long legs of extinct animals. "We're in a fairy tale," she announced. Littering the bark of a dead pine were sacs of fur from which, Raymond told her, caterpillars had burst into miracles called moths. His father taught life sciences. Jocelyn, whose mother birded, said that the gold of a finch is money in the bush. She glanced down and said, "Are you circumcised?"

"Can't you tell?"

A squirrel spied upon them. "Sure I can. Winston is."

Winston, frightened, caught up. "Shhh," he said, his whole face an alarm bell ready to ring. He had heard something, maybe even seen something.

"Like what?" Raymond said.

"A person."

"Let's get out of here," Jocelyn advised in the instant.

Running lickety-split, they bashed through inky swarms of black flies smearing the air, dodged stray skunk scat, slashed through ferns, and made it back to where they had chucked their clothes. Hands high on her hips, Jocelyn toed her garments, sifting, sorting, and abruptly her alert eyes narrowed. "Something's seriously missing."

Her white cotton underpants.

Dr. Wall told her to focus on memories that mattered. These came to mind:

Her mother plucks a tomato from the vine and eats it warm and un-washed, an act so thrillingly primitive that Jocelyn snatches one for her-self, richly ripe but blemished as if from a bug bite. "Eat it, dear," her mother says. "Imperfections make life real." She is five, and her mother, lovely and patrician, is all-knowing.

At Logan International she glimpses a man's face like that on an ex-pired passport photo, the face younger than it has a right to be. All the same, she calls out, "Raymond!" And the man stops in his tracks and says, "He was my father." Of course. Raymond is in the ground, for years now.

At a party in Boston's Back Bay her mind is slush, for she had pur-posely drunk too much. A spill puts her on the floor, her underpants a swamp. She has thoroughly wet herself, which humiliates Winston. A moustache notwithstanding, Winston has the face of a well-behaved child accustomed to having his head patted and his bottom wiped. "I'll call a cab, that's the most I'll do," he says. She waves a helpless hand. "I don't think I can get up." He angles his face. "Not my problem."

In her sophomore year at the academy, English Comp, she wrote a story about a passionate woman who seduced a snowman in a neigh-bor's yard. The snowman gave the woman frostbite while melting in her arms. It was a parable about the dangers of venereal disease, but Mr. Helms, Winston's father, didn't get it or didn't want to and gave her C-minus. Mr. Helms considered her insufferably brainy and a crea-ture of privilege who expected special treatment because her blue-blooded father was headmaster. The next week she composed a paper about a man molesting his son's teddy bear, and Mr. Helms promptly returned it, the grade written in red. *Garbage!*

Winston said, "My father says you're a show-off."

She squinted an eye. "I yam what I yam. I'm Popeye the sailor man."

Her favorite teacher was Mr. Pryce, head of the English department, lean, taut, and boyish-looking, on whom many of the girls, including herself, had fierce crushes. Fetching in school colors, jacket maroon and skirt and knee socks cadet gray, she sat in Mr. Pryce's cramped office in Fraser Hall. He knew why she was there and spoke before she could. "The answer's no."

"Why not? I'm smart enough." She wanted to switch from English Comp to Creative Writing, which Mr. Pryce taught only to seniors. "Please, Mr. Helms is a pill."

"You're not asking for special treatment, are you?"

"God, no!" she said. "But something you should know. I'm in love with you." Gazing at him, she imagined an exchange of open-mouth kisses of the sort she shared with Raymond, his hands like Raymond's on her cuppy breasts. "If people knew my fantasies, you could go to jail, Mr. Pryce."

"Then I'll definitely grant you no special favors."

She knew he was divorced and, as far as she knew, had no known close female friends. "Are you homosexual?"

"No, Jocelyn, merely human. So I watch my step. Especially with faculty brats."

She was Dr. Wall's favorite patient, he her first shrink, and that was long ago. Her flaxen hair had faded, the doctor's glasses had thickened. Smiling ironically, she said, "We've grown old together."

On his desk were period pictures of children who had since crept into middle age. New clients mistook them for grandchildren. "I believe we have."

She was deep in the leather chair facing his throne of a desk. On his first visit she had suggested sitting on his lap. If he could've seen his face. *A joke, for God's sake!* He was paralyzingly serious back then, not a trace of the boy in him, the boy apparently bound and gagged at an early age.

"You look glum," he said, with eyes ready to console. He had always been infatuated with her and imagined traces of her lipstick on words meant solely for his ears.

"Friends can be disloyal," she said. "They die."

"It's what people do, Mrs. Duhamel. They live briefly, then die for-ever."

"No need for brutal truths."

"You used to demand that from me."

"I was young, which made all the difference in the world. Young, you can weather anything." Her face went dull. "I'm all alone, Harvey."

He once considered her cavalier use of his given name disrespectful but now found it endearing. Were their roles reversed, he would tell her of a suicidal moment in medical school when he gulped pills and had to be pumped out. "Ultimately each of us is alone," he said.

"That's a truism. I'm paying you good money to be original."

Dr. Wall had a ton of love for her, she had not an ounce for him. He had something to tell her but wanted to wait until the end of the session to begin preparing for the little divorce. Like a little death. He decided not to wait. "I'm retiring soon, Mrs. Duhamel. My wife and I are moving to Florida."

"Florida? How unimaginative." Taken by surprise, she was angry and a little shaken. "I don't appreciate being abandoned."

"You're not being abandoned. I'll refer you to someone I'm sure you'll be comfortable with."

With a sudden thrust forward, she was out of the deep leather chair and, though still on the clock, set herself to leave. Dr. Wall rose awkwardly from his glossy desk to walk her to the door. Aging had left him squat, as if heavy hands had pressed down upon him. His full head of wiry gray hair was staticky. Opening the door, he gazed into her face, probably the last time he'd see it. She brushed by but immediately glanced back.

"I'll need your number in Florida."

Mr. Pryce, usually clad in a tweed jacket and chino pants, had on a pilly sweater with the sleeves pushed up to the elbows. Jocelyn said, "Well, what did you think of it?" Her latest offering in Creative Writing concerned a devout young man who dreamed he had sex with his minister's wife, whose looks were lovely, God's generosity. Ashamed, he confessed to the minister, who forgave him and passed the confession on to his wife. She immediately phoned the young man and said, "How was I?"

Mr. Pryce had the story on his desk. "Interesting," he said, "but it doesn't go anywhere."

"Does it have to?"

"I'll let you answer that."

She was only a few months away from Radcliffe, the Cambridge scene, Harvard Square, a mere hour away but a world apart from the cocoon of the academy. "Will you miss me, Mr. Pryce?"

"Probably. You're an imaginative young woman, and I think you're going to be somebody."

"I'm already somebody." She imagined taking charge, throwing a leg over him, grabbing the reins. She took a quick breath. She needed to. "What was your wife like, Mr. Pryce?"

"Like you."

"I'm a romantic."

"I know."

The gallop winding down, she pictured herself falling asleep in the ache of his arm, a literary conversation on tap when she woke. She rose slowly, books pressed to her chest. "You harass me, Mr. Pryce."

"I *what?*"

"In my fantasies." She tossed her hair. "Raymond gets jealous."

"Might be wise if you kept some of your fantasies to yourself."

Raymond was waiting outside Fraser Hall. Her first lover, he stood six feet in a button-down shirt open at the collar and jeans tight at the crotch, with a forelock sweeping his brow. Impatience heightened his voice. "You were in there long enough."

"Don't pout." She rose on tiptoes, bathed his face with spearmint breath, and kissed him hard enough to push him back a step. He reached out, touched her.

"Marry me."

"What? Don't be silly."

He would be leaving for Stanford, clear across the country, while she stayed in Massachusetts. "I don't want to lose you."

Adorable Raymond had tears in his eyes. She told him she'd think about it.

Dr. Wall took her call and murmured, "More memories?"

"Questions. How much of a person is pure banality?"

"I suppose it varies."

Under the weather, she spoke from a raw throat. "I don't want to be banal. You'd tell me if I were, wouldn't you?" She didn't hear his answer but was confident it was a nod. "Another question. Am I original?"

"Everyone is. Up to a point."

"Are you humoring me?"

"I wouldn't dare."

She glanced out the window and felt the dark day shudder. Freezing rain was expected. "How's Florida?" She didn't want to know. "Strike that."

"What's wrong, Mrs. Duhamel?"

She edged closer to the window. "Last question. "Why can't the mind give itself a day off?" Hearing nothing, she sensed a shrug.

She found Radcliffe a breeze, a fun thing. Harvard Square types pursuing her included an aspiring actor on the verge of becoming someone else, a visiting Greek scholar fluent in broken English, and a pot-smoking painter who said her breasts glowed like Cezanne's apples. Eventually each came up short. The actor's lines grew stale, the scholar's knowledge of antiquity proved shallow, and the painter struggled with mediocrity. The only touchy time was when she was careless with one of them and found herself counting on the calendar until the morning she startled her dorm mate, Nanette, with a whoop.

"Oh my God, what luck! What grand fabulous luck! I'm having my period!"

"Men are fine—in their place," Nanette offered.

A week later she and Nanette lay together, though how this happened was unclear to her. Nanette's voice dampened her ear. "This is not for everybody." She relished the experience but wondered whether the idea of adventure was greater than the deed itself. And she was of a mind that romantic love lacked weight. Any breeze could blow it away.

She read Giuseppe di Lampedusa, who defined love as "flames for a year, ashes for thirty," and she gorged on foreign films. Her favorites were *Hiroshima, Mon Amour* and everything by Fellini, especially *La Dolce Vita* in which Marcello Mastroianni set the gold standard for men, Anita Ekberg paraded her wares, and Tarzan, an aging hunk, played himself. The *Transatlantic Review* published her short story about a couple who had their differences. The woman was introspective and subtle, the man basic, high-handed, and loud. Imagination set her free; cold intelligence had a lock on him. He had a blunt tongue, she an incisive one. They were *Cat and Dog.* Payment was thirty dollars. She graduated near the top of her class, a degree in English literature and a job offer from Houghton Mifflin. Editorial assistant. Read *glorified secretary.*

"I'll take it," she said.

Dr. Wall wasn't in. His wife took the call. What was her name? Violet. Vivian, Vicki. Something like that. Jocelyn switched the phone from one ear to the other and said, "When will he be back?"

Mrs. Wall wasn't sure. "Probably around three. He's playing only nine holes today. The heat, you know."

"No, I don't know. Tell Harvey I need to know how much of life is hearsay. Just a little or a whole hell of a lot?"

Mrs. Wall pulled in her breath. "You understand the doctor is retired."

"Which doesn't stop him from cashing checks I send him. Just tell him to call me. Will you do that, Vicki?"

Another tug of breath. "My name is Vera."

Promoted within the year, she was given a small office with a partial view of the Common and traffic on Tremont Street. Her first author, a best-selling biographer making a stab at fiction, was legally blind, his eyes tarnished coins, his work dictated and transcribed into a weighty manuscript that lay on her desk. She had read every word.

"Well?"

"I need to be honest, Lionel."

"Of course. May I call you Jocelyn?"

She stared at his hard serious face and saw something of a Tartar in the height of his cheekbones and the slant of his devalued eyes. Paraphrasing Mr. Pryce, she said, "Creative writing is like lovemaking, Lionel. A tender caress is more sensual than a grab below. Subtlety is supreme. In plain English, Lionel, one wants to balance a smile with a teardrop, a truth with an absurdity, a curtsy with a fart."

"I see. Figuratively speaking." Light glanced off the blades of his face as he shifted in his chair. "Is the damn thing publishable? Just tell me."

"We'll work on it. If it wasn't good, I wouldn't bother. We'll trim fat and loosen the collar of your clergyman. By the way, I like him. Good character."

They labored for three months, many cuts, much rewriting, and came up with a product that held God accountable for defects and demoted man to an animal with an attitude. The protagonist was a priest who in the final scene served a wafer with a dab of cheddar, relegating himself to a waiter and Jesus to a tidbit. Jocelyn chose the title. *God's Game.*

"Wasn't supposed to be comedic," Lionel said.

"Life usually is. At first glance." More from Mr. Pryce. "Tragedy lies between the laughs."

Released a year later, the novel received good reviews and went into a second printing. They celebrated with dinner at Maison Robert. "Your name should've been on it too," he said. "More your book than mine. Are you this wonderful with all your authors?"

"Only if they're blind in one eye and can't see much out of the other."

"Look, I really mean this. I want to share royalties with you."

"I'll tell you what." She poured bubbly. "Why don't you marry me instead?"

Jocelyn spoke into her cell, an edge to her voice. "Is he avoiding me, Violet? Did he not get my last check?"

"We don't need your money. We're quite comfortable down here."

"Land of the living dead. Ladies with rosy-veined legs. Jesus, Violet, get a life."

"We have one, thank you very much."

Jocelyn drew a sharp breath. "I think I understand. Harvey wants to wean himself from me."

"You have it backwards, Mrs. Duhamel."

Difference in age didn't matter. Nor did his disability. His hands cruising the curving surfaces of her body were his eyes. He wanted to *see* every bit of her. During the honeymoon breakfast he asked what logic had led them to the altar. She said she relied not on logic but epiphanies. They had been married for less than a year when she lost him. Cane in hand, he raised it high, and stepped into Tremont Street traffic. From her desk she heard sirens, then, though wailing sirens were not uncommon, heard herself scream.

It was a bad year that got worse. Her father suffered a stroke that reduced his tongue to baby talk. A second stroke erased him. "A blessing," Winston's father whispered at the chapel service. She had never liked Mr. Helms and found herself liking him less. After the service she drew Winston aside and asked about Raymond, and he told her what he thought she already knew. Raymond had married a California beauty, fathered sons, and was doing well for himself in the land of sunshine and navel oranges.

"And you, Winston, what are you doing?"

He worked only a walk away from Houghton Mifflin. Managing money, moving funds, high-stakes stuff. Not the field he thought he'd be in. He stood soft-looking and prissy in a vested suit, his hair flat, formal, and precisely parted. "We must get together," he said.

She looked for Mr. Pryce but learned he was on sabbatical. Europe, her mother said. Her mother retained use of the headmaster's house while a search committee went about its business. Jocelyn said plaintively, "You didn't plant tomatoes this year."

"Many things I didn't do this year. Or ever will again."

She needed to get away and asked her mother to join her on a Mediterranean cruise. Her mother wasn't emotionally up to it, so she went alone, manuscripts in her luggage. She was at the rail when the ship passed the Italian waters where Shelley had drowned. A woman standing nearby said, "Excuse me, I saw your name on the seating list. You aren't by chance related to the author Lionel Duhamel?"

"My husband," Jocelyn said. "He's on a different ship."

Dr. Wall came on the line, which surprised her, irked her, and amused her. "Are you playing games with me, Harvey?"

"I would never do that." His tone hovered between professional and personal. "But you need to know you're upsetting my wife."

"She'll live. Life is too short not to."

Dr. Wall's voice deepened. "Don't send any more checks, Mrs. Duhamel."

"Really? I notice you cash them." She was seated by a window, dead of winter, wine warming her head and blending with melancholy. "A question, Harvey. Do our tracks in the snow substantiate our existence?"

"More or less."

They sat in a bar-lounge midway between the State Street brokerage firm where Winston worked and Houghton Mifflin where Jocelyn now had a larger office and an assistant. "Yippee for me," she said and jostled the ice in her whiskey sour, which was twisting its way to her head. She reached across the table and touched his face as if she were a nurse, he a patient. "I'm trying to remember, Winston. Are you circumcised?"

He colored. "Of course."

"Why of course? Raymond isn't. Last time I looked."

"Is this a conversation we need to have?"

"Not if it makes you uncomfortable." Piped in was Peggy Lee's *Is That All There Is?* She sighed. "So cynical. So sad. Makes you want to cry, doesn't it?"

"No." He sipped Perrier and glanced openly at his watch, which she ignored. When the waiter approached, he placed his palm over the mouth of his glass, and she gestured for another. "But you haven't finished that one," he said.

"But I will. You can count on it." More Peggy Lee wafted through the air, this time all dressed up with a broken heart. "The driver who killed my husband was never charged. Got away scot-free. Another injustice, Winston. You never met Lionel, did you? He had the sort of face that could've been handsome but didn't know how. You'd have liked him."

She gazed off, as if into the clouded past. "I've loved only two men. Lionel and Mr. Pryce."

Winston looked surprised. "You must've loved Raymond."

"Not mind and body. Only body. When we were kids, you and Raymond were my men. Those were sweet times, Winston. Why haven't you married?"

"Too busy."

A fresh whiskey sour stood before her. Suddenly she didn't want it and didn't need it. "I see a shrink, Winston. Regularly. I highly recommend him."

"I don't need a shrink."

"Look at me, Winston." Her eyes showed purpose, her voice took command. "I lost a father, a husband. Now I need a brother."

She phoned Florida and learned that Dr. Wall was hospitalized. "My God, what happened?" A heart attack, she was told. Recovering nicely, with a stent freeing one of his arteries. Prognosis was positive. She expelled a sigh of relief. "Please, Vera, tell him I'm pulling for him."

After a noticeable silence, Mrs. Wall said, "Do you realize that's the first time you've got my name right?"

Winston lived in the upper reaches of a waterfront condo complex that Jocelyn found depressing—too damn neat, too fussy, the furniture and drapery more appropriate for an old maid with money. She visualized his horror were she to drop crumbs on his carpet, leave a water stain on one of his mahogany end tables, or break one of his crystal curios picked up in Ireland or Italy. "In some ways, Winston, I bet you're much like your father."

"I'll take that as a compliment."

"Don't."

She lived in a book-cluttered second-floor walkup on the wayward side of Beacon Hill. It was where she and Lionel had lived, Lionel's place before it was theirs, now only hers, though some of his personal items and large-print books remained. Winston felt uncomfortable, as if walking in another man's shoes, and went about on tiptoes to avoid disturbing a ghost.

"For God's sake, relax," she said. "Better yet, go home."

Nanette, her Radcliffe buddy, survivor of two bad marriages, joined her for a Saturday lunch at the Parker House. Nanette raised both a wineglass and her voice to announce she'd had her fill of men. Heads turned. "Up to here!" She sliced a fast finger across her throat. In a normal voice Jocelyn proposed a worthy substitute. Winston. "Don't do me any favors," Nanette pleaded.

Winston didn't like the idea either. "Don't try to fix me up," he said.

"Learn to let loose a little," Jocelyn said.

"Leave me alone."

As a last resort, she took him to bed. He was chalky white. "You need sun, Winston. A lot of it."

He was on her, barely moving, as if he needed a push. Still bearing his weight, she sensed their bodies coming to a slow understanding. "You love him, don't you?"

"Who?"

"Raymond."

"You had a scare," she said.

Dr. Wall agreed. "Indeed I did."

"In the hospital did you pray?"

"No."

"Good for you, Harvey. Eventually some super computer will unsmear the universe and expose God for what he isn't."

After ten years at Houghton Mifflin she left to write short stories and soon had enough for a collection, which Little, Brown published. The opening story, written after Winston told her Raymond had terminal cancer, questioned how much appreciation, if any, an undertaker receives from the corpses he serves. The concluding story, a dozen in all, involved a woman much like herself who, unaware she's in a footrace, catches up to her future and becomes one with her past. The collection, dedicated to the two loves of her life, received good reviews and earned back her advance. She drove to Kenwood Academy, carried a copy into Fraser Hall, and greeted Mr. Pryce in his office, his hair grayer than she remembered but everything else about him the same. She dropped the book on his desk.

"Maybe you've already read it."

He claimed he hadn't, not yet, but she believed he had, hoped he had. In a burst, she told him that she wrote solely to impress people meaningful to her, and he certainly was among the biggies. "I'm flattered," he said.

"You should be. You of course know you dominated my schoolgirl fantasies. I gave you lots of chances, but you never acted. Why not, Mr. Pryce? Was I too young for you?"

She didn't think he was going to respond, for he swiveled in his chair and stared out the window. "You weren't too young, Jocelyn. You were too old."

His words raced beyond her brain but at once circled back and let her grasp what she never would have guessed. Her face burned. "All these years I thought it was Winston's father. But it was you."

"Am I supposed to know what you're talking about?"

"You know exactly what I'm talking about, Mr. Pryce. Do you still have them?"

His eyes turned away from her as if her face had overstayed its welcome. "No, Jocelyn. You outgrew them."

Returning to Boston, she drove too fast and nearly got into an accident changing lanes on I-95. Relief was Sumner Tunnel sucking in traffic, her Honda part of the debris. Another lovely sight was the murk of harbor water when she pulled into a parking area near the condo complex Winston called home. She had amends to make and drummed her fingers on the keypad when he took his time buzzing her in. The elevator was a whiz through time. Seated in his spacious living room with its scenic view, though at the moment there wasn't much of one, she said, "I need a drink." All he had was Absolut. Fine. With orange juice. "I apologize," she said. "To you and your father."

"For what?"

"I'll tell you sometime. Or maybe I won't." She finished her drink quickly and considered having another. "I want you to take me to a party tonight. I promised my editor I'd be there."

"I'm not one for parties."

"Make an exception. I may need your help." She stared at him. Losing hair on his head, he was cultivating a moustache, not much of one. "Do you know what lies between ages eleven and fifteen, Winston? A world of difference."

Surprise of surprises. Dr. Wall called her. "We were worried," he explained. "Been a while since we heard from you."

"I've been busy, Harvey. Writing another novel. One of the characters is a fellow like you, same head of hair, same bowtie. The angel of death taps his shoulder and says 'I don't think we've met.' Scary, huh?"

"In that context, I'd say yes."

"If you die, Harvey, promise me you'll come back."

"I'll do my best."

Nanette married for a third time. "Why'd you do that?" Jocelyn asked, and Nanette said she wasn't young anymore. Jocelyn didn't believe one had anything to do with the other and said so. "And a bit of advice if you don't mind." Promptly she recited a line from a novel she was writing. "The sum of a man is always subject to subtraction."

"You can say the same thing about a woman," Nanette retorted.

"Absolutely not." Again she plagiarized herself. "Women face the facts of life and death with more fortitude than men. To a man, mortality is not natural. To a woman, it's just one more thing to cope with."

The novel sold well or well enough. Hopes had been higher. Her editor at Little, Brown, his asymmetrical face as pleasant as it was disconcerting, said, "You know I love everything you write, but perhaps if you were less gloomy sales would broaden." She said she'd take it up with her characters, who were not always of a mind to do her bidding.

"They can be stubborn."

"Like you."

Jocelyn's mother was living on Cape Cod with her second husband, a retired physicist who on her last visit told Jocelyn that every action has a reaction, but not every action deserves one. He had changed since the last time. With weight loss, his eyes were taking over his face. Jocelyn murmured, "You're losing him, aren't you, Mom?"

Her mother, harvesting tomatoes, said, "He believes in probabilities with the exception of one certainty. Yes, dear, I'm losing him."

At Logan Airport, returning from a long weekend in New York, she glimpsed the past. Raymond? Couldn't be. It was as if they were shuttling through overlapping time zones reckoned in years, not hours. She spoke his name, not loud, and he stopped dead in his tracks. Raymond, once removed, made her want to cry. She hoped Raymond *père* had had a caring undertaker who fixed him up pretty for the big show. Raymond *fils*, spit and image, even had a flop of hair across his forehead. She wanted to kiss and hug him. For old times. But there was no time. He was headed one way, she another.

Her editor at Little, Brown went through her next manuscript, *Love is Blind*, smiling at times against his will, and called her into his office to tell her so. She said, "Yes or no?"

He said, "Maybe."

A WOOLF IN VITA'S CLOTHING

Ten years ago a man named Benson married her and took her to North Dakota, where gigantic skies diminished her, winds haunted her, and winters oppressed her. Her only means of escape was a Greyhound bus. People in the town called it "riding the dog." She rode the dog to Chicago, arriving with forty-four dollars in her bag, which was a weight because much of it was in coin.

In a coffee shop she chose to sit beside a man who appealed to her in a comforting way. He had the sort of face, not entirely unattractive, that looked as if it wanted to be forgiven, the sin left to the imagination. At other moments, however, when he gazed at her over his coffee mug, she sensed something unexplained and inaccurate in his face.

Eating a blueberry muffin, the first food she'd had since boarding the bus, she said that the greatest loneliness in the world resides in North Dakota, the loneliness limitless in winter and hellish in summer. The roads, she said, were made for high speeds and suicides, the suicides usually called accidents.

"I've never been to North Dakota," he said.

She told him that her husband owned a stereo, which he tuned to farm reports in the morning and country music at night. Their only child, a son, she said, died before his second birthday. From her weighted bag she produced a color snapshot of the child.

Glancing at it politely, the man said off-handedly, "So, you've left your husband."

She returned the picture to her bag.

"You're a good-looking woman," he said, staring intently at her. "He might come looking for you."

"No. He won't do that."

"How can you be sure?"

"I'm sure," she said.

Later he took her to a hotel, where she soaked in a hot bath and then wrapped herself in a voluminous towel. He was sitting low in a chair and watching television news. Suddenly he gripped the arms of the chair and sat erect. "Jesus," he said. "That's you!"

She peered carefully and critically at the screen. "I wish they hadn't used that picture."

He was looking at her in a whole new way. The color in this face had risen. "Why did you do it?"

"Do you need to ask?"

He thought for a moment. "No, I guess not."

"Are you going to turn me in?"

He used the remote to kill the television. "I suppose I should, but I won't."

She let out a breath. "I don't know your name."

"Chuck," he said.

She held out a hand. "I'm Caroline."

During the night he woke with a start, raised himself on an elbow, and peered down at her in the light from the bathroom. In sleep she looked imaginary, a product of whatever dream she was dreaming.

In the morning he ordered breakfast for them through room service. She stayed in the bathroom until it was delivered. Over coffee he said, "You should dye your hair."

Her hair was very blond. "No, I like it as it is."

"Then tie it in a knot or something."

"Yes, I can do that."

"You can't stay in Chicago."

"I don't know where else to go."

The morning paper had come with their breakfast. He refrained from looking at it. "We'll think of something," he said, rising. His suitcase was of dark leather and fully packed. Hers was of cracked plastic and contained changes of underwear and little else. "We'll have to get you some different clothes," he said.

"Are you rich?"

"I have credit cards."

Her bag was on the dresser. He felt the weight of it when he moved it and wondered whether the weight was a gun. Opening it he saw a load of coins. He took out a handful for the maid.

She kept pace with the fast sidewalk crowd. Newly outfitted in navy and white—a jacket with outsize lapels and pockets, a blouse full of frills, and a skirt billowing from the hips—she came across as the sails and rigging of a slender ship braving rough waters. The eyes of a derelict went small looking at her.

She waited at a corner, where the air of traffic stood tall. The springtime sky had a summery touch. A crowd waiting to cross compacted around her and then, when the lights changed, hurried on without her. Presently Chuck arrived in a gray rental and flung open the passenger door.

"Get in."

Several blocks later they got snarled in a gridlock at an intersection. It was almost as if a malignant force were binding them in. She looked out her window at a man maneuvering a shopping carriage brimming with redeemable cans. She gazed past him to a window of dinette furniture.

"I was born in this city," she said.

"Do you have family here?"

"Nobody. My mother and father are dead."

"I like your outfit."

"It's not me," she said.

They did not speak again until they were free of the gridlock and nearing an artery that would take them out of the city. She said, "Where are we going?"

He said, "We'll know when we get there."

Road-weary, they checked into a motel off a highway in Indiana. Again she had a long hot soak in the tub, as if to steam away not only North Dakota but Chicago. When she emerged in one of his shirts, he was watching television, which did not surprise her.

"Was I on again?"

"Only for an instant," he said, viewing her with sober eyes. "You should've bought some jeans. We'll get you some in the next town."

"I'm running up a bill."

"I don't keep chits."

She stepped behind his chair and gazed down into his hair, which held a few threads of gray at the part. "Chuck," she said in a near whisper.

For a moment he did not respond. Then he did, quietly. "What?"

"You haven't told me anything about yourself."

When he closed his eyes and remained silent, she moved to the television and scrutinized the pay offerings. "They have dirty movies," she said. "I've never seen one."

"Do you want to?"

"No," she said.

In bed, the light in the bathroom left on, he made love to her with her consent but without her full attention. She would rather have turned over and gone to sleep. When he finished, she was wide awake. Lying on her side, facing him, she began talking about her husband, how she had managed it. He was sleeping, she said. When she cut his throat, she saw a quart of blood.

"I don't want to hear," he said.

"I'm sorry."

He lay still. "My wife is dead."

"Like my husband?"

"No, it was different."

She waited for him to go on, but he did not. Soon he was asleep, and eventually she drifted off. In a dream her husband's corpse came to life and went crazy over the condition it was in.

They stopped in a small town in Ohio for lunch. She had on a white blouse and jeans, and she wore her hair in a severe bun, which gave her face a broader definition. They lingered at the restaurant to the point that the other tables began to stand empty. Without prompting, he told her he had taught literature at Dartmouth College, where he had met his wife, a graduate student of uncommon abilities and diverse opinions.

"I knew you were educated," she said.

He sipped his coffee. "We were married twenty years."

"Did you love her?"

"Very much, but it's not clear whether she ever loved me."

"Did you have children?"

"Two boys, grown now. They hate me."

"Do they have reason?"

"They think so," he said and fell into one of his silences, which threatened the air between them.

"Please," she said, "tell me what's going on in your mind?"

"You don't want to know."

"But I do."

"A drama," he said, his tone turning light. "Vita Sackville-West, handsome in men's clothing, is having tea with Virginia Woolf. Virginia places a hand on Vita's trousered knee and says, 'I wish I had your balls.'"

"Are they real people?"

"They were real once. They're mythology now."

"I'm not sure what you're telling me."

"My wife left me for another woman."

The waitress dropped off the check. She wanted to pay it, but he took it from her and laid out a gilt credit card. She said, "Did you kill your wife?"

He smiled thinly through the dark of his face. "There were two trials, mistrials, deadlocked juries. They finally let me go."

"Tell me about your sons."

"I already have. They hate the ground I walk on. They testified against me. They raged at the district attorney when I was freed." Without warning one of his hands began to tremble. Instinctively she reached over to steady it, but he drew back. "It'll pass," he said.

The waitress processed the credit card and returned it. He scratched his name illegibly on the receipt and managed a smile. Moments later, from across the room, the waitress gave them a hard stare.

"Let's get out of here," he said.

Springtime sleet fell in upstate New York. Chuck squinted through the windshield, for the wipers were smearing what they plowed. On the interstate, after paying the toll with quarters from her bag, he drove at a moderate speed, and she counted mileposts along the way.

"Why are you doing this for me?" she asked. "You probably could get any woman. You don't need me."

"We need each other," he said. "I saw that right away."

Within the hour the sky cleared and the sun came out. The defroster had made the air in the car humid. Her white shirt felt clammy against her skin. She felt she had gone bad in it.

Chuck said, "How did you meet your husband?"

"He came to Chicago. He wore a tan suit. It was summer, and I was clerking in a convenience store."

"Why did you marry him?"

"He put his hand over his heart and said he loved me."

They passed a disabled car squatting in the breakdown lane. The sun, wheeling in and out of clouds, showed itself in momentary shocks, as if someone were shooting at them. She lowered the visor.

"When things went wrong at the farm he blamed me. Some things were my fault, but I did my best. He said my head was in the clouds."

Chuck's eye was in the rearview. "Reality craves fantasy."

"When the baby took sick he wouldn't call the doctor. He didn't believe in doctors, only in God. He was a church-goer. I'm sure all the people at the church hate me now."

"Yes, you can bet on it," he said abstractedly.

"Is something wrong?"

"There's a police car behind us."

"I'm not scared." She raised the visor. "Why aren't I, Chuck?"

"You haven't come down yet. In time you will, and then you'll be scared of yourself."

"How do you know?"

"I know," he said.

Watching starlings descend like a rock slide onto the grassy center strip, she thought of people at the church. The only one she would miss was eccentric Mrs. Hager, who wore wide-brimmed hats and smoked while she prayed.

Chuck's voice loosened. "It's gone," he said.

Turning, she glimpsed the state police cruiser veering around the curve of an exit ramp.

They checked into a motor inn in the Berkshires. He had bought her a nightgown with lace. Humid from her bath, her backside was a rosy glow inside the gown. She pulled at the elastic on his boxer shorts and let it snap against his skin.

"That hurt," he said.

She apologized in a soft voice. "That wasn't my intention."

From the bed they watched one of those movies, her idea. She thought it might be fun. A nun lifted her skirts and revealed long splendid legs. Then a man came into the picture. The mole on his back looked like a penny.

Chuck spoke in her ear. "Turn it off if it offends you."

"No," she said. "It's what people do."

He said, "There's nothing people won't do."

After the movie was over he propped himself on an elbow and seemed to find something wondrously pristine about her body, as if no hand other than her own had ever touched it. He bared her breasts appreciatively, as if removing gift apples from their tissue wrappings. Some women are unforgettable in their nakedness. He told her she was one of them.

After they made love they lay locked in the dying intensities, with neither wanting to let go. He stroked her hair. "I hope I'm wrong," he said, "but this may be our last night together."

She breathed up at him. "Why do you say that?"

"I've been foolish about money. It's added up to quite a bit. They're after me too."

She embraced him harder. "We've become close."

He said, "I love you, Caroline."

"Are we still in Massachusetts?" she asked.

"New Hampshire," he said.

Here in New England the sky seemed closer, the clouds pushed low, not at all like North Dakota where the heavens are gigantic, the clouds massive and aloof, and the emptiness awesome. She remembered storms so horrendous they threatened to crack the planet.

"Are you scared yet?" he asked.

"No," she said.

He was driving on back roads and finding excuses to stop in each small town they came to. The strong scent of potpourri issued from a gift shop. He went into it and bought her a silver bracelet, a perfect fit for her slim wrist. At a small shopping center he picked out a stylish trench coat with slash pockets and a wide belt. She looked quite nice in it.

"Why do you keep putting me in different clothes? Are you trying to make me someone else?"

"You are someone else," he said.

"I feel like I'm in the movies."

Back on the road she stretched her legs out as much as she could and dozed off. In a dream a fully uniformed police officer, the brightness of his brass vying with the shine of his leather, tapped her solidly on the shoulder and said, "Are you Caroline Benson?" Pointing at Chuck, she said, "You'll have to ask him."

At nightfall he reached the end of the line, a town where landmarks evoked memories and raised ghosts. The Texaco station was a beacon. Blue neon burned over the doorway of Bill's Café, a hangout for rural riffraff. He could see into the drugstore, which was stuck in time. It had a marble soda fountain and round revolving seats. The soda jerk was in his nineties.

He drove through the center and past the lights of the library, where forsythia was in gushing bloom. Caroline sat with her head back and her eyes closed, but he knew she was not asleep. As he neared the far edge of town the roadside went wooded. Headlamps of an approaching car were pale strains adhering to nothing, and the car, which may have been a van, floated by without sound or shape, driverless for all he knew.

Warm air from the day clashed with the cold of evening, and swirls of mist ran yellow in the moonlight and hovered ghostly wherever the road dipped. He drove with a fear he might hit something, for the road was rerouting itself the way a river sometimes abandons its bed to make another. Then the road straightened, and he knew exactly where he was.

Caroline said, "Why are we stopping?"

"You grew up in Chicago," he said, "I grew up here."

He stepped from the car, waited while she buttoned her trench coat, and then gave her his arm. The moon irradiated a path that took them through the pinewood and the ring of peepers. A pond opened in front of them.

"I used to take my boys fishing here. We never caught anything but perch."

"I've never seen a perch," she said.

"They're not very big."

They stood at the edge of the pond, mist scaling off the surface, the moon mirrored on it. The moon fascinated him. It was a dead thing that looked alive on the water. It was gloom wearing bridal white. He said, "We grow, we reach a height, we contract, we die. Ever ask yourself why, Caroline?"

"Yes," she said. "When my mother died."

"Beautiful stars up there," he said, raising his eyes. "What we see as up could be down."

"How can we tell?"

"We can't. Think of God as a mathematical genius and a perverse toy-maker. Who else would have put worlds spinning on their axes? Leaves us not knowing which end is up."

"But he must have done it for a purpose."

"Pure amusement, Caroline."

"You're fooling me," she said. "Tell me what you really believe."

"At some point the universe will dissolve into an idea of itself, from which it evolved. Put another way, when God grows bored with his idea of us, we're finished."

She tightened her grip on his arm. "That can't be true."

"Truth is relative. A lie told in Chicago is gospel in North Dakota."

"You know so much."

He wanted to tell her that he knew nothing. He was a product of group therapy, disturbed strangers bathing in a communal pool of unhappiness polluted by self-pity, their troubles traced to others, not themselves, responsibility seldom mentioned.

Passing geese skimmed their shadows over the water and eclipsed the mirrored moon. Dark air currents carried the scent of pine. "I'm getting scared," Caroline said. The moisture of night sheathed her face the way it did apples in an orchard. "What's going to happen to me, Chuck?"

"We devise our own punishment. A woman I mentioned, Mrs. Woolf, waded into a pond like this one and never came out."

"I wouldn't want to do that."

"Nor would I," he said and led her from the water's edge.

In a country inn a mile from the pond she shrugged off the trench coat and said, "You were wrong. We have another night together."

"We got lucky," he said.

The room was unlike the others they had shared and gave her an uneasy sense of being back at the farm. The furniture could have been acquired from an old funeral home. A high-back chair stood somber and still, the arms rubbed smooth as if by grieving hands. A settee issued a prayerful air of rectitude. Decorous endtables and a dropleaf desk stood stolid. The only thing missing was a sampler on the wall.

"It's like you've brought me back," she said.

"I've brought us both back."

"Why?"

"We can face anything together."

In her mind the room was not here but where it should be. The sampler appeared on the wall. Fascination held her eyes open. A blink would have exploded the image.

"Yes," she said when he kissed her.

He undressed her and told her she was lovely everywhere. On the bed he kissed the soles of her feet. No man had ever done that to her before.

"Yes," she whispered. "I love you too."

They rose late and checked out after a slow breakfast. The air was warm, but the sky threatened. When they climbed into the car they saw sprinkles on the windshield. He did not drive far, only a few miles beyond the inn. Pulling over, a grove of birch and maple in sight, he let the car slow to a standstill.

A fine rain netted trees and veiled shrubs. The grass steamed and wet her shoes. Violets lay cool in their foliage. She hiked the collar of her trench coat and took his arm. He had on a nylon jacket and sturdier shoes.

"I used to bring the family here," he said. "Picnics."

In the grove they passed tables and benches. She could hear the light rain in the trees, the sound like metal points pricking the leaves, which were tender, not yet at full strength. There were trees in North Dakota, but she could not remember any of them.

Leaving the grove, they climbed over a low crumbling wall of unmortared stones and stepped into a meadow. A single magnolia in full bloom gave her a sense of being a bride again. Beyond the meadow was a grassy hill, over which they saw a small slash of lightning. "This isn't the best place to be," he said.

"I don't mind, if you don't." She reached for his sleeve. "Do you believe in God, Chuck?"

"I don't believe anything can come from nothing, so there must've always been something. That's as far as my mind will take me."

"I believe there has to be something other."

"That's a whole new ballgame," he said and gazed toward the hill. "Will you climb it with me?"

The gray sky darkened as they crossed the meadow. The rain weighted their hair but not their steps. When she glanced at him, her smile resembled his, giving them a fleeting physical likeness. Seen from a distance, they looked cut from the same hide.

At a roll of thunder he glanced back as if something had been lost. She gazed ahead as if much were to be gained. On his mind were things no longer worth telling, on hers matters too complex to mention. He heard another roll of thunder and imagined it chasing him. She believed it was leading her. Climbing the hill, he believed nothing more was at stake, and she believed everything was. He expected to die and be nowhere. She anticipated an elsewhere.

At the top of the hill they held hands and let go at the vital moment. Surging from the sky like a white shark, the bolt of lightning struck her and missed him.

She had won. He had lost.

Driving back through the town, he considered seeing his sons but didn't want to shock them.

Later, the sun brilliant, an elderly couple with birding binoculars found her where she had fallen, her trench coat scorched black. Her bag, split open, was a spill of coins.

PLUM ISLAND

I don't know his name. He never said it. Nor did I mention mine.

I've seen him here before, this hour of the day, the sun sinking, ebb tide, and on this same spot on Plum Island, where he stands apart from the other fishermen, who look like fishermen. He doesn't.

They have the proper poles, the right gear, the special caps and hats, while he is dressed in gray, the pants from an old business suit. His rod and reel seem too flimsy for the surf.

They stand with cool detachment and sealed lips. From time to time he tosses his weight from one leg to another. They stand still. Sand fleas bite him but not them. They rear back to cast, and the snap and whistle of their lines are like guns fired at human targets. They show no emotion. He does.

He reacts sharply to things. The sudden slap of a wave. The kick of the wind so that the sand stumbles. The sudden appearance of birds in the sky, like scratches on glass. The formation of a tidal pool, a glittering ghetto of broken shells, washed-up weed, fish bones, and a single fish head with its eye a gem in all that junk.

They socket their poles in the sand and lounge next to them like warriors resting their weapons, their faces plain. His is deluged with detail, ornate in its architecture, with its high forehead, spider web wrinkles, prominent nose, thoughtful eyes, and split chin. They are young compared to him. He may be eighty, or more.

They come to fish, semiprofessionally, with no enthusiasm, as if they knew in advance they would catch old fish, sluggish stripers. He comes for other reasons, which I figure out for myself. He comes to brood over the beauty of the place, to study the ancient history of the scroll-like sea, to stand in the pea-green dusk and ponder waves that wear out before reaching shore.

I figure he's from Newburyport or Rowley, perhaps Salem or Ipswich. None of these places. He's from Boston, he says. Some years ago he used to come here to Plum Island with friends whose names now escape him, fishermen who spoke little, grunted much. "Not unlike these fellas around us."

And years before that, he says, he came here with a woman whose child collected sand dollars and wanted to spend them at the store. His voice softening, he says he wanted to marry the woman and would have if things had been different. How different? He doesn't say. Now he doesn't know where she is, probably in the ground.

He and I have difficulty threading our hooks through sandworms, which aren't worms at all but insects with teeth like those of mice. You have to grab them behind the head so you won't be bitten. He is not careful, and he makes a thin pointed sound, almost like a toy whistle, as he tries to shake off the pain.

I tell him that I've seen him before.

He laughs. "Maybe you only think you have. Old geezers look alike."

"No, it was on this beach, right here. Maybe a month ago."

"Possibly," he concedes.

His thoughts return to the woman he didn't marry, to the way she stood near the surf and rearranged her mass of hair so that he could better see her face, which was small and fine-boned, like her hands. He recalls how she dropped her hands from her hair and drew her child close because of a sudden figure on the beach, a man with a shotgun held downward, laid against his leg.

"Tell me more."

"Nothing to tell. He was just there, an omen, a presence you couldn't ignore. At least she couldn't."

Darkness arrives quickly. We can no longer see where we have cast our lines. Nearby a fish is making its final argument with a hook baited by one of the other fishermen. The old man wonders aloud about the guilt of a fish that gives itself up so easily.

"Listen," he says and tells me about the woman's child, a boy of four, who buried a dead bird and exhumed it a day later, upset because it hadn't risen. Then he talks about the woman's face, which eventually gave out a silent message. "Ask me anything. I have no answers."

He speaks with such quiet force that I can see the woman, her bones truly fine, just as he said, and I can hear her voice, which is dry and resigned, unvarnished. Then she grows aware of my eyes and vanishes into the past, where moments, hers and mine, no longer connect.

He and I catch nothing. I expected to, or at least hoped to. He asks where I live. I tell him. Andover. He's quite familiar with it. He went to the academy. He asks whether I'm married. I am. He asks whether I have children. I do. Daughters.

"Then you've caught something," he says and smiles. "You won't go home empty."

His face changes. In a snatch of moonlight it now reminds me of a business seal, drawn particularly tight at the mouth, above which, I notice for the first time, is a moustache of sorts, a rigid row of short silver hairs, mandatory for men of a certain age and station.

He reels in his line. No bait left on the hook, which is how he wants it. He separates the pole into two pieces. His box of sandworms is mine if I want it. He must return to Boston. Here at Plum Island, where things become lost forever in the sand or washed away with the tide, the world is ageless, all of a piece, fish and fisherman one, the fishermen interchangeable, ghosts of other generations. He and I are one, our age difference blurred.

The others have gone, as if they had never been present, and now he is leaving, briskly for a man of eighty or more. Something he says stays in the dark.

"Carry on, son."

©KEVIN HARKINS

Born in 1932 in Exeter, New Hampshire, Andrew Coburn has lived most of his life in towns outside Boston. Following US military service, he joined a local Massachusetts newspaper, launching a career as an award-winning crime reporter and bestselling novelist. Nominated for the Edgar for *Goldilocks*, the third novel in his Sweetheart Trilogy, Coburn has been translated into fourteen languages and was awarded an honorary doctorate of letters for his service to journalism and the novel. He lives in Andover, Massachusetts.